Through a blur of tears, she saw his head bending toward hers. . . .

But there was no menace in his aspect. His face was softened with pleasure as he smiled at her. His lips alighted on hers, gently as the brush of a butterfly's wing. His arms closed around her, still gently, but the kiss deepened.

Francesca felt she was in a dream. Devane was going to rescue her. He loved her. His arms tightened, and she put her arms around him, returning the pressure. The embrace quickly escalated from tenderness to rising passion. Suddenly Devane was crushing the air out of her lungs, and Francesca was shocked to notice that she was reciprocating. She drew back, breathing hard, and embarrassed.

Also by Joan Smith
Published by Fawcett Books:

LADY MADELINE'S FOLLY
LOVE BADE ME WELCOME
MIDNIGHT MASQUERADE
THE MERRY MONTH OF MAY
COUSIN CECILIA
WINTER WEDDING
ROMANTIC REBEL
THE WALTZING WIDOW
THE NOTORIOUS LORD HAVERGAL
BATH SCANDAL
JENNIE KISSED ME
THE BAREFOOT BARONESS
DANGEROUS DALLIANCE

FRANCESCA

Joan Smith

FAWCETT CREST • NEW YORK

A Fawcett Crest Book
Published by Ballantine Books
Copyright © 1992 by Joan Smith

Library of Congress Catalog Card Number: 92-90147

ISBN 0-449-21845-7

Manufactured in the United States of America

First Edition: August 1992

Chapter One

Lady Camden, known as Frankie Devlin to her *intimes*, made a final turn in front of the mirror before leaving for her evening's pleasure. The deep blue of her gown, tinged with violet, just matched her eyes. The gown was cut daringly low, revealing the incipient curve of creamy bosoms. Her raven tresses were arranged in the careless-looking *victime* do, in a tousle of curls around her pale face. Too pale! She returned to her toilette and carefully spread rouge over her cheeks. God, only twenty-five, and already she was resorting to the rouge pot to enhance her complexion! It was all these late nights—but one had to have some pleasure from life after all, and at least she slept after a late night.

A shadow appeared at the door, and an elderly lady entered. She was tall and lean, with her graying hair bound in a white cap. Her eyes went to the mirror, settling with a frown on her niece's low-cut gown. "Who are you going out with tonight, Fran?" she inquired.

"Major Stanby," Frankie replied over her shoulder.

Mrs. Denver essayed a tense smile. "Major Stanby again, eh? This is beginning to look serious," she said hopefully.

Lady Camden carefully avoided looking at her companion. "He is just a friend, Auntie. Pray don't go imagining any romance in it. One marriage was enough." Her thin voice suggested one had been more than enough. "Major Stanby will be returning to the Peninsula any day now."

"Where are you going this evening?"

Lady Camden hunched her insouciant shoulders, revealing more of the creamy bosoms than Mrs. Denver liked. "Out. I don't know. Stanby said to bring a domino, so perhaps we'll stop in at the Pantheon."

A hand flew to Mrs. Denver's lips. "The Pantheon! That is not quite the thing, my dear. One hears gentlemen take—er—lightskirts there."

"They also take ladies, carefully masked. Don't worry. And please don't wait up for me, Auntie. I may be home late."

Mrs. Denver shook her head at the reflection in the mirror. How had sweet little Fran turned into this—well, perhaps "hussy" was too strong a word, but "fast" was not. "These late nights are beginning to tell, Fran. You've lost weight—though I must say your color is still good."

Lady Camden carefully palmed the rouge pot and slid it into her reticule. No point shocking poor Auntie. "Why, thank you, ma'am. Late nights agree with me, you see. And now I am off."

With a wave of her fingers and a flutter of blue silk, Francesca flew out the door. Mrs. Denver looked after her sadly. The poor girl was running as hard as she could, but there was no escaping the past. When word was first received from the Peninsula that Lord Camden had been killed, Francesca turned into a ghost. The death was so unexpected as to seem incredible. Camden wasn't even an officer, but a civil servant sent over in a liaison position between the military and government. It had seemed a safe appointment, though Francesca had begged him not to go.

Married only six months. It was an odd thing for Camden to take the post, but then, he was a fly-by-night sort of fellow, never satisfied with anything for long, including his marriage. It was a dark day when Camden went into Surrey and captured the heart of Francesca Wilson, a simple country girl who had never been six inches off the leash. She hadn't a chance against his charm, good looks, and title. The couple were married within two months, against the better judgment of both families. Camden whisked her off to London for the gaiety of her first Season. Her letters home had been full of joy and wonder. David had arranged to have her presented at court; she had met the Prince of Wales and attended balls and parties and the theater. It must have seemed like a dream to simple Francesca.

And then as suddenly as he had married her, Lord Camden had sailed off to Spain and been killed. If Fran had only had a child, she might have borne up better under her trials. She was made of stern stuff, and even the death she would eventually have mastered, but the other ... That was when she turned into this hellion who cared no more for propriety than she cared for a flea.

"If it is lightskirts gentlemen prefer to their wives, then so be it. I shall have a dozen flirts, and enjoy myself as David enjoyed himself," she proclaimed when she had assimilated her husband's infidelity.

Mrs. Denver remembered the day Francesca found out the truth, that her darling groom had been carrying on with fast women from the second month of their marriage. Fran hadn't realized it all the time they were married, nor for six months after they received the death notice from Whitehall. It was a Mrs. Ritchie, acting under the guise of a friend, who had told her.

"Poor Francesca, how we miss that dear boy of yours. He was the life and breath of all our parties. Did he ever tell you about the duel he fought over Cynthia, the pretty little actress at Drury Lane? He used to hang about the green room like a puppy, waiting for her to appear and toss him a bone. Of course the gentlemen didn't shoot to kill. One does not *die* for a lightskirt, after all, but it was rather a nasty shoulder wound he received."

Francesca hadn't said a word. She just stared, as if the sun had fallen from the sky. Mrs. Denver remembered that shoulder wound, ostensibly sustained in a hunting accident. It happened the month she came to stay with her niece and Camden. David was "so busy" at Whitehall in the evenings that he wanted Francesca to have a woman with her. Now she knew what "work" he had been up to, and so did Fran.

One could hardly blame the girl for cutting up a little. She had been so madly in love with David. Once her eyes were opened, she soon tumbled to it that the Drury Lane actress was not his only mis-

4

tress. She had found the key to his locked desk, unlocked it, and gone through his papers with a fine-tooth comb. She found enough in the way of billets-doux and bills for jewelry never received by her that there was no denying the truth. The man was a confirmed rake and libertine.

Francesca went about like a statue for a month, then anger seeped in to replace disbelief and sorrow. She was young. Her life was not over. She would enjoy what was left of it. As soon as the mourning period was over, she had set off on a spree that threatened to ruin her reputation as well as her health. No gown was too daring, no party too déclassé, no spree too wild for Frankie Devlin. She despised her title and encouraged her friends to call her Frankie. What she really wanted, Mrs. Denver thought, was to be a man, with a man's freedom. She had adopted a hard surface sheen that hid all the hurt inside. This month her flirt was Major Stanby, a war hero.

"But what is he like?" Mrs. Denver had demanded when the major rose as a favorite.

"Monstrously handsome, Auntie. Everyone stares when he enters in his scarlet regimentals. All the ladies are mad for him, I promise you."

"I don't mean his *looks*, Fran. What of his character, his estate?"

Francesca gave that shrug her aunt was coming to loathe. "Men have no character. He is handsome, and amusing—and not demanding."

This last was tossed as a crumb. Her major did not insist on the full privileges of a lover. So far as Mrs. Denver knew, Francesca had not yet sunk to having adulterous affairs, but it would happen sooner or later if she continued carrying on in this loose fashion. Mrs. Denver's sole support and consolation in all this troublesome business was Selby Caine. He had known Francesca from the cradle, and kept an eye on her as best he could.

He called that evening at nine, as he usually called every evening, and Mrs. Denver met him in the Blue Saloon. It was not a large chamber, nor a very elegant one. Lord Camden's father, Lord Maundley, owned the small house on Half Moon Street, and lent it to Camden and his bride when they came to London. Maundley had suggested she remove to his own mansion on Berkeley Square when David left for Spain, but as his appointment was for only three months, she had kept the house instead. She would never go to live with Lord and Lady Maundley now, leading the sort of life she led. They would be scandalized. Indeed, they already were scandalized. The only communication with Lord Maundley was his monthly visit to Half Moon Street. His wife had gone into a decline upon hearing of David's death, and did not leave her house or receive visitors.

Mr. Caine stepped in and made his bow. He was a modest country gentleman of medium height, brown hair, sepulchral eyes, and an austere face. He was still a bachelor at thirty-seven, but had no romantic interest in Francesca. He was more like a brother than anything else. Francesca and Mary Travers, his sister, had been friends forever, back in Surrey. They had stood bridesmaid to each other, and still corresponded, though Mary's match had not been so great as her friend's.

"How did she seem tonight?" Mr. Caine asked gravely. He had the unsettling habit of standing throughout his visits, and weaving back and forth as he spoke, like a reed in the wind.

"Do have a seat, Mr. Caine." He ignored this. "She seemed the same as usual. Determined to be happy, you know, but not really anticipating much pleasure, I think."

"Pleasure is not to be found in the sort of society she keeps. Did she say where she is going?"

"Perhaps the Pantheon—she took a domino." Mr. Caine gave a heavy sigh and began weaving to and fro. This performance always reminded Mrs. Denver of her one sea voyage, during which she had endured agonies of nausea. She felt the echo of it now.

"With Stanby again?" The dame nodded. "She could hardly be in worse company. A soldier on leave, out for a good time. I doubt she will escape this encounter unscathed. The Pantheon is the haunt of the most dissolute libertines in all of London—and Fran is there with a soldier on leave."

"Stanby seems a sound enough fellow. Young, of course, and madly in love with her."

"I doubt he has marriage in mind. If he hasn't a dark-eyed wife waiting for him in Spain, it is more than I know." His weaving accelerated.

"I cannot believe that of him, but in any case, Fran has no thought of marriage."

He drew a deep, forlorn sigh. "And why should she, after her experience? The best to be said for her seeing an officer is that he'll be leaving town soon. God only knows who she'll take up with next. We'll live to see her abandoned, with a houseful of kiddies and no money to rear them. Any chance of her returning home to White Oaks?"

Mrs. Denver tried to ignore his dark prognostications. "I doubt it. She seems determined to make a name for herself. Just as well she does it here, and not disgrace her family back home."

"When the Season is over, she might reconsider, though it would be hard for a woman used to the fleshpots of London to go back to a house like White Oaks, and be under her father's thumb again. They live a simple, retired life there. Fran isn't used to that now. I don't know what will ever come of her, Mrs. Denver."

"Nor do I," the lady answered in a dull tone. She watched Mr. Caine weaving and offered him a seat again.

"I must go after her and see if I can ward off utter disaster. The Pantheon, you said?"

"Amongst other places. You would know better than I, Mr. Caine."

"I know too well," he said in a voice of utter doom. He left, and Mrs. Denver took a novel to her room to try to forget for a few hours the awful fate awaiting her charge. Mr. Caine was so kind and helpful that she felt guilty for disliking him.

Major Stanby's carriage drew to a stop in front of a classical building on the south side of Oxford Street. Lady Camden adjusted her blue domino and entered the Pantheon proudly on the major's arm. Whatever the place's reputation, it certainly struck the eye as the height of opulence. Chandeliers scattered random rainbows of color on the gilt interior and the multicolored dominoes below. Music wafted out from the dance floor. A gratifying number of friends greeted them, and total strangers ogled the handsome couple—the officer in his scarlet regimentals and the elegant lady in blue.

Francesca cast off the lingering misgivings her upbringing plagued her with and told herself she was happy. It would be divine waltzing with Arnold. Everyone would stare at them. As soon as she had a few glasses of wine she'd shake off these blue devils and be fine. The major led her to a table in a sequestered nook and ordered champagne.

Candlelight flickered on his half mask, on his lips, lifted in a smile, on a flash of white teeth. "To us," he said, and touched her glass with his. She drank thirstily, emptied the glass, and held it out for a refill.

"Now, don't get tipsy on me, Frankie," he said playfully. "The night is young—and I have something very important I want to ask you before it is over." He filled her glass, and she sipped more slowly.

He's going to ask me to marry him, she thought. Oh, dear! She had feared it might come to that. Arnold was a nice man. She didn't want to hurt him. "Let us dance," she said, trying for an air of merriment.

"Yes, but before we do—" His hands came across the table and touched hers. She hastily withdrew, seizing her glass as an excuse. She lifted it and drank again.

"Don't say anything serious, Arnold," she said gently. "Let us just enjoy our last few evenings together."

"But I shall be leaving the day after tomorrow."

"I know. And I shall miss you. It's been fun, hasn't it? I hope you've enjoyed our little friendship."

"Friendship!" he exclaimed in astonishment.

"Let's dance," she repeated, and rose.

9

Stanby hoped the waltz might accomplish that softening in his companion that champagne had not. He held her close, their posture duplicated by other couples under the anonymity of masks and dominoes. She felt his warm lips on her forehead, and something in her congealed to annoyance. She pulled back, but he soon held her tightly again. Before any further maneuvers were accomplished on either side, the music stopped and they returned to their table. From the corner of her eye, she spotted Selby Caine, her guardian angel, and breathed a sigh of relief. If worst came to worst, she was at least sure of a safe escort home. She nodded at him. He nodded back gravely but did not approach her. Strange, how he always brought the air of a funeral with him. Even at this rowdy place he looked to be in mourning.

Lady Camden did not notice the tall man standing in the shadows beside Selby observing her performance and would not have recognized Lord Devane if she had seen him. Devane did not move in her late husband's raffish circle. In society, he resided at the very tip of the ton, which did not prevent him from visiting such haunts as the Pantheon. He wore a sardonic, anticipatory smile. He had been on the point of departure, but hesitated. The lady in the blue domino looked interesting. A new lightskirt this Season. He quietly moved closer to the table where the major and Francesca had been sitting.

Once they were seated, the major would no longer be put off. "Darling, I must speak," he said in loverlike accents.

"I won't hear it, Arnold."

"After all we have been to each other? You let

me kiss you—ardently." His voice was high with disbelief.

"A few kisses don't mean I want to *marry* you. I am too old for you. I have been married once already. Your family would despise me."

"There is no reason they need know till the thing is done," he said eagerly. "We could get a special license and be married before I sail."

Francesca made the error of trying to persuade an infatuated man by logic. "What would be the point, for just one day? You could be gone for years, and where would I live while you are away, Arnold?"

"Why—with Mama and Papa, in Yorkshire. Once we are married, they would have to accept you. It will only be for a few years."

She adopted a world-weary tone, to let him know this line of talk was hopeless. "In Yorkshire? But, my dear, what sort of social life do people have there, so far away from London?"

"Why, we visit a dozen families."

"A dozen families! My, my. You are active."

Stanby felt a flush rise up his neck. "Not what you are accustomed to, I daresay, but—"

"Not at all what I am accustomed to, and not what I intend to become accustomed to. If you cared for me, you would not ask me to give up all my friends and pleasures and rusticate for years, alone, with your disapproving family."

"Then why have you been leading me on?" he demanded, becoming sulky.

She looked away and saw that Selby was still hovering near the door. It would be best to cut this friendship off now. A quick cut was less painful in the long run. "Because you used to be amusing. You

11

are rapidly becoming a dead bore, however, so I shall leave." On this curt speech, she rose, picked up her reticule, and left.

Major Stanby was not two steps behind her. Between drink and frustration, he scarcely knew what he was saying. He only knew that the most wonderful woman in the world was turning him down after encouraging him wantonly for three weeks. He grabbed her elbow and whirled her around. "Frankie, don't leave like this."

She read the hurt in his voice, and though her heart was heavy, to encourage him would only prolong his pain. He was a man; he wouldn't hurt for long. "Let go of my arm," she said coldly, and twitched away. He grabbed both wrists.

A dark form detached itself from the shadows. Before the major knew what was happening, his arm was pulled from Francesca's elbow and twisted cruelly. "The lady said no," Lord Devane pointed out coolly. "Are you a gentleman, sir, or only an officer?"

Francesca turned to her helper. "Oh, do be careful! The major has a wounded shoulder."

Devane's fingers fell at once. He leveled a menacing eye on Stanby and said, "Let us not make it necessary to wound the other one."

"Do run along, Arnold," she said. "It is no good, you know. I'm sorry if you misunderstood."

Major Stanby's youthful lips curled into a sneer. "Just as you say, madame, but I must offer a word of advice. Further misunderstandings are bound to occur if you are so free with your favors." He made a very stiff bow and left, hot tears stinging his eyes.

His friends had told him Lady Camden was trouble, and they were right. He was somewhat re-

lieved at not having to marry behind his parents'
back. What on earth would they have made of
Frankie Devlin? But she would be something to remember, and tell the chaps about when he was back
in the Peninsula.

Chapter Two

"Shall I go after the whelp and teach him some manners?" Lord Devane inquired in a voice of silken menace.

"No, let him go."

Francesca lifted her eyes to observe her rescuer. She saw a well-shaped head with carefully barbered, crow-black hair. His upper face was concealed by a black mask, revealing only a glitter of dark eyes, but his thin lips left an impression of arrogance. He wasn't a young man; there were incipient lines in his swarthy cheeks. She recognized the work of Weston in his elegant black jacket and a taste for finery in his intricate cravat, a cabochon ruby nestled in its folds. He was tall and athletic in build, with broad shoulders. "I am obliged to you, sir," she said, and turned to leave.

The hand that shot out to detain her wore a carved emerald ring on its small finger. Its grip was firm to the point of severity. "Give him a minute to clear away. He may be waiting."

His voice, though quiet, was deep and full of authority. It was the sort of voice that did not have to be raised to gain attention. Who could he be? He was right about Arnold's possibly lingering outside. It was exactly the childish sort of thing he would do. She really must graduate to more urbane flirts, she told herself. These boys were becoming a bore. "May I offer you a glass of champagne, sir?" she suggested, indicating the table, where a half bottle still remained.

Champagne, indeed wine of any sort, was not the reward Lord Devane had in mind. In any case, he would never drink another man's leavings. But he was in no hurry. He enjoyed the preliminaries of love as well as the main event. He lifted his hand, ordered a fresh glass and a new bottle of wine. "I prefer port. You finish the champagne," he said, holding her chair.

As soon as he was seated, he pulled aside his mask. "I have nothing to hide, have you?" he said, hinting for her to follow his lead.

Francesca felt herself being subjected to a frank, searching gaze from a pair of eagle eyes that lifted the hair on her arms. A slash of black brows lent her rescuer a menacing aspect. She touched her mask but didn't remove it. Devane glanced at her left hand, and saw her naked third finger. She had cast the ring aside when she learned of David's infidelity. Single ladies of quality did not come to such dens as this. She was therefore a lightskirt, and a demmed pretty one, to judge by those cherry lips. Her chin was small and somewhat pointed. He was eager to win a smile, to judge her teeth. He always took an interest in a filly's teeth. He had noticed her lithe form and dashing gown some minutes before, while she was dancing. "Well?"

15

"I really shouldn't be here," she said nervously. His raking gaze set her on edge.

"I won't tell anyone if you don't. What is your name?"

After Arnold's somewhat scandalous exit she had no intention of revealing her true identity. "Biddie," she said, reaching into the distant past for her baby name.

"Biddie what?"

"Wilson." Her maiden name could mean nothing to him. "And whom am I to thank for rescuing me?"

He noticed her accent was good, though somewhat countrified. Perhaps an actress, hoping to play a lady at Covent Garden? "Devane."

A little gasp caught in her throat. So this was the great Devane! She recognized the name from the journals and conversations overheard here and there. Devane was not in the government—she had some vague thought that he was a prominent Whig. She knew that a title attached to him, but couldn't recall whether he was a duke or marquess, or perhaps an earl. "My—friend was somewhat impetuous," she said apologetically.

"A woman must be a little careful of her friends."

"Yes."

The port and glass came, and they drank without speaking for a moment. "The major leaves for the Peninsula in a few days," she said to fill the stretching silence.

"And he wanted some pleasant memories to take back with him," Devane said insinuatingly.

She disliked his tone, and the direction of the conversation. "He wanted me to marry him," she said.

Devane's lips moved in silent derision. "And who

16

shall blame him? The Dragoons are known for their excellent taste in ladies." After how many bottles of wine had the fool suggested marriage—if he had suggested it?

"He's very young," she said, and gave her characteristic shrug. Devane's eyes lowered to her partially revealed bosoms.

"Not younger than you, surely? You don't look more than—" He hesitated. With her eyes hidden, it was difficult to judge, but certainly she wasn't hagged. Her jaw was firm and smooth.

"Oh, I am very old," she said, and laughed. A silver tinkle echoed on the air. She felt a hundred, but as her companion's lips moved unsteadily, she realized that she was not so old as he. He must be well into his thirties. Some feminine vanity urged her to point this out. "Perhaps not compared to you, but I am no longer a deb. I am a widow, in fact."

He discarded this boast without even considering it, since she wore no ring. It was odd she admitted to being older. Devane said, "Take off your mask." It was a politely worded command, and such was the force of his personality that her hand actually moved to do as he bid.

She checked herself, however. "A lady in my position shouldn't be here, in a place like this. It was foolish of me to come."

"We all act the fool from time to time. I am feeling foolish tonight myself. Shall we have a dance?"

"I really should be going."

"You can't go home alone."

"I have a friend here." She looked around the room and spotted Selby at his post, watching her with glum foreboding. She waved to him. Devane

17

looked, and caught a glimpse of two women at the doorway near Selby.

Her bland mention of being with a friend was all the confirmation he needed that she was a light-skirt. They traveled to such places as this in pairs or groups if they were not escorted by a patron. "You see now why I refused your offer of wine. I wished to keep you in my debt. Come now, a lady always repays her debts. I have rescued you. You owe me one dance."

"Well, just one," she said, and rose, eager to have it over with. It had been a dreadful evening. Mrs. Denver would be happy to see her home early, for once.

They were playing a waltz. Waltzes featured prominently at the Pantheon, to allow the patrons greater freedom. In fact, so many of the couples were inebriated that the formality of a minuet or cotillion would be beyond them. Devane led her to the floor, where jostling and rowdy customers elbowed them mercilessly. It seemed like a sort of gentlemanly protection when Devane held her closely in his arms.

But as the dance neared its end, the idea that he was any sort of protector at all was banished. "Why don't we get out of here and go someplace where we can be alone?" he said bluntly.

She stiffened in his arms. "I really must go!" she said, and darted from the floor. She ran back to their table to grab her reticule. He was hot at her heels. "Are you feeling ill?" He had noticed her drinking her wine too quickly, unless she was a confirmed drinker so early in her career.

"I must go!" she repeated.

"What's the matter? Do you already have a patron?" he asked baldly.

Although she was familiar with the word, it was confusing to hear it used in connection with herself. "What do you mean?"

"I mean, are you already spoken for?"

"No—that is, I told you I am a widow."

"Then, what is the problem, Mrs. Wilson? We'll go to a quiet, private inn. I know of a place on the Chelsea Road."

There was no longer any possibility of misunderstanding his meaning. He had mistaken her for a lightskirt. Selby had often warned her of that possibility, but she never paid him any heed. She felt thoroughly ashamed, and was too modest to be angry. Her only wish was to escape before he learned her identity. This Devane was persistent, however, and highly effectual. She would have to use guile to be rid of him. "Well then, why don't you have your carriage brought around while I powder my nose," she said with an enticing smile.

She received an answering smile of triumph. "Five minutes, at the front door." He left, and Francesca beckoned to Selby, who immediately joined her.

"Get me out of here! Devane is having his carriage sent around. He thinks I am going with him."

"Does he know who you are?"

"No."

"Good! Come with me."

Mr. Caine took her hand and they skirted the room till they found a corridor leading to the rear of the building. They left by a side door, and walked along till they met a hansom cab. As they drove home, he took the opportunity to give her a stern lecture. He was doubly miffed that he would have to come back later and recover his chaise.

"What happened with the major?"

"He took the stupid idea he wanted to marry me, and wouldn't take no for an answer. Devane sent him packing, and then I had to try to get rid of *him*. But he can't possibly know who I am."

"Didn't he ask your name?"

"Yes, I told him I was Biddie Wilson. Oh, I wish I *were* Biddie Wilson again," she said petulantly.

"But you're not, my dear. You are a lady, and it's time you began acting like one instead of inviting such disasters as this by behaving like a hurly-burly girl. That was Lord Devane you were with."

"He told me his name. What has that to do with anything?"

"He flies too high for you, Fran. A man like that— you couldn't manage him as you do your younger flirts. Devane means business. It is exactly what I have been warning you about these past weeks."

Francesca felt a blush suffuse her cheeks. She didn't tell Selby what Devane had suggested; it would only increase his wrath, and the length of his lecture. A frisson of fear scampered up her spine as she recalled Devane's cold, dark eyes examining her. "He has no idea who I am. He is not part of my set. I'll stay well away from him if I see him about anywhere."

"You would be well advised to do that. Your being a widow would be no protection against a man like Devane. I don't say he'd go after a maiden, but a widow is as good as a harlot to the likes of him. He flies with the highest, fastest set in town."

"I wonder why I was never presented to him when David was here," she answered tartly. "They sound like birds of a feather. The very sort of gentleman I despise."

"And the very sort you will attract, carrying on as you do. Haven't you had enough of playing around, leading a life of dissolution, Fran? Nothing but grief will come of it. If you won't go home, for God's sake, find a decent husband and marry him."

"Then *I* will be bound leg and wing, and *he* will continue playing around! No, thank you."

"Well, at least keep out of Devane's way."

A lecture was always enough to set Francesca back in fighting mode. "Do you know, Selby, I don't think I shall go home just yet after all. It is only ten o'clock. Let us go to some rout or other instead."

"I am taking you home," he said sternly.

At the corner of Bond Street and Piccadilly, Francesca recognized a friend's carriage. She pulled the check string and hopped out. "Thank you, my guardian angel. Don't worry. I shall be with the McCormicks." She blew him a kiss and ran to the other waiting carriage.

Selby drew a deep, defeated sigh. Well, at least it was the McCormicks. They weren't as bad as most. He had introduced Fran to them himself. Selby's own circle of intimate friends knew his concern for Lady Camden, and assisted him in watching over her. Alfred McCormick wouldn't let her run off with anyone undesirable. He called to the driver to take him back to the Pantheon, where he recovered his carriage and drove to Brooke's Club to finish the evening with a game of cards, if he could find anyone willing to play for chicken stakes. Mr. Caine was not the man to plunge into unrestrained gambling.

Francesca threw off her domino and mask and attended a small rout party, where she met a circle of her own flirts, and had a noisy evening of dancing and laughing and drinking a little too much wine.

It was not the sort of do to attract Lord Devane. He waited five minutes in front of the Pantheon, and when Mrs. Wilson did not come out, he went in to look for her. He toured the hall once, then returned to his table. He was more curious than offended, yet more angry than curious. Why had she run off on him? He was the answer to a light-skirt's prayer. Wealthy beyond the dreams of avarice, fairly generous, amusing. He was no Adonis, but no one had ever called him ugly. In return for his manifold assets, he demanded a semblance of breeding from his mistresses, and Mrs. Wilson certainly had that. He demanded constancy, of course. One did not buy a chicken to provide other men omelettes. And in return he provided a residence, a clothing allowance, cash, and a reasonable amount of jewelry.

Perhaps she was ill? A gentleman like Lord Devane was not left alone at such a den as the Pantheon. Within two minutes he was joined by a female acquaintance who had her eye on him. Peg Clancy was very pretty, but she was a common, garden variety harlot who held no interest for Devane. He asked her to see if there was a Mrs. Wilson in the ladies' room. She skipped off and returned in a minute.

"No, she isn't there."

"Have you met Mrs. Wilson? A new woman in town."

"Can't say that I have."

"Black hair, a good accent."

"The lady you was waltzing with?"

"That's the one."

"Coo, you never mean she done a flit on you!" Peg laughed uproariously. "She's a new one to me. She couldn't've known who you are."

"If you can learn anything about her, write me a note to this address," he said, and handed her a card, accompanied by a gold coin. "There'll be another one to match it when I hear from you."

"Lud, I can't write. Drop around tomorrow night and I'll tell you what I've found out."

"Fair enough."

He left, and Peg beckoned her friend, Mollie, to come and help her finish a nearly full bottle of port. "Know anything about a girl calling herself Mrs. Wilson?" she asked.

"Harriet Wilson, you mean?"

"Nodcock! As if Devane wouldn't know *her*! No, this one is younger, and pretty. Ask around. There's a bob in it for us if we find her."

At the end of the evening, however, nothing had been learned of the mysterious Mrs. Wilson.

Chapter Three

The weekend arrived, causing a brief cessation of festivities in the Season. Francesca thought often of Major Stanby. He would be leaving the next day for Spain, perhaps never to return alive, poor boy. She wondered how long he would remember her. The harsh outlines of Lord Devane's face obtruded often into her consciousness, too, but she made an effort to forget him. He was precisely the sort of gentleman she despised. The only difference between him and David was that Devane made no effort to conceal his character, but then David had probably not bothered either among his low female friends. She wondered if Devane had a wife; if he had, she pitied the lady.

On Monday afternoon she drove in the park with Mrs. Denver, where she met friends and arranged her evening's schedule. They would attend the new comedy at Drury Lane and stop off at the Listers' ball afterward. Francesca had her own theater box, and as there was a seat left over, and as Selby had been so kind to her, she invited him to join them. He would be the ghost at the feast, she feared.

As she prepared for the evening, her thoughts were all on making a grand appearance and attracting a new beau. She wore an emerald-green gown that emphasized her large, wide-spaced eyes. Its rich color contrasted dramatically with her creamy throat and arms. The bodice clung to her high bosoms and fell in graceful folds, causing a feminine rustle of silk when she moved.

"I wish David had left my jewelry with me when he went to Spain," she said to Mrs. Denver as she finished her toilette. "I have only this shabby string of pearls to wear everywhere." Mrs. Denver knew she referred to the entailed jewelry and did not bother mentioning David's wedding gift of diamond earrings, bracelet, and brooch. Fran never wore them. She kept them in her bottom drawer, so she wouldn't have to see them and remember.

The pearls gleamed luminously against her skin but were hardly visible at a distance. Francesca took up a colored paste brooch and attached it as a pendant to the necklace.

Mrs. Denver shook her head in condemnation of this freakish idea. It looked decidedly odd, yet it would probably start a new fashion. Francesca had a knack of creating fads. She had single-handedly revived the *victime* coiffure that had come into fashion along with the French Revolution. That same brooch that now hung from her necklace had appeared on her gloves two weeks before, and the idea had been taken up by a dozen foolish ladies. Another time she had taken to wearing her rings outside her gloves. Mrs. Denver looked askance at a patch box on the dresser, hoping her charge did not intend to start wearing patches.

"The jewelry is entailed," Mrs. Denver reminded her. "It will be for David's brother, when he marries."

"As Horton is only seventeen, I cannot think he will want it for a decade. I would ask his papa for it, if Maundley weren't such a stick." As she spoke, Francesca opened the box and extracted a small black patch. She tried it at the outer corner of her left eye.

"Don't, Fran, you'll only make a cake of yourself," Mrs. Denver said. "It is ill-bred to try for attention by these tricks."

"Have you seen my fan, Auntie?"

Mrs. Denver went to the bed for it, and while her back was turned, Francesca stuck the patch on the inner curve of her bosom, planning to transplant it later. She hastily put on her pelisse, to hide the stunt from her aunt.

Mrs. Denver enjoyed a relatively carefree evening knowing her charge was with Mr. Caine with whom she would suffer nothing worse than boredom. No harm could come to her at the theater, and they would be there for most of the evening. Major Stanby was gone; it would take Fran a few days to find a new flirt for them all to worry about. If only she could care for Mr. Caine—but then, he was so dull, poor lad, and given to those tedious sermons. He ought to have been a bishop.

Francesca was scarcely aware of Selby as she adjusted her opera glasses to scan the boxes at the theater. She had forgotten to move the patch from her bosom. She observed several ladies checking out her new brooch-necklace and smiled to see Miss

Frobisher remove a brooch from her glove and attach it to her diamonds, where it looked quite ghastly. Miss Frobisher was a regular sheep. She was still wearing a brooch on her glove when that had been out of fashion for two weeks. Several of Lady Camden's followers were still wearing rings outside their gloves.

She did not observe Lord Devane lurking in the shadows at the back of a box across the hall, his glasses trained on her. He recognized that tousle of black curls, and those impertinent shoulders at a glance. Discreet inquiries in various quarters had turned up no knowledge of Mrs. Wilson, though several had queried whether he meant Harriet Wilson. A coincidence that Biddie had used that name, or was it an announcement that she meant to be the Season's reigning courtesan? He thought it an excellent jest, if jest it was. He liked her insouciance, too, in wearing a patch on her bosom. He recognized it for a patch. He had seen enough of her bosoms the other evening to know they were unmarred, snowy white. Did the patch on the left side indicate that she was a Whig?

If the girl was clever and venturesome and ambitious enough to be inventing her own trademarks, it seemed unlikely she hadn't recognized him the other evening. She had tipped him the double to increase his interest, and ardor. Damme if she hadn't succeeded. His glasses moved to examine her friends. That nondescript, sad-eyed gent—hadn't he been with those girls Mrs. Wilson waved to the other evening at the Pantheon? What was the relationship between them? No matter, she would drop him soon enough if the dibs were in tune. She'd want a good allowance, a house, a carriage. . . . These were reasonable demands and caused the wealthy earl no undue concern.

His lips curled in amusement; then his glasses rose to examine Mrs. Wilson's face. He was delighted to discover she was even more beautiful than he had imagined. The shade of her eyes was not discernible from the distance, but he could see they were large, wide-spaced, and dark. Her nose was straight, with just a suggestion of a tilt at the end. She had called herself "an older woman." She was no girl, but hardly old. Twenty-four or -five. He preferred the experience of an older woman in his affairs.

Devane had attended the play with his sister, her husband, and his family, the Morgans. Marie would not take it amiss if he left them after the play, and Lord Morgan would be delighted to be allowed to return home directly to bed. In fact, he was nodding off already. Devane decided he would follow Mrs. Wilson's carriage when she left, and discover where she lived. There was no point asking Marie if she knew anything about Mrs. Wilson. Lady Morgan would scarcely recognize the name of Harriet Wilson, the most infamous courtesan since Nell Gwynne. Marie knew all the respectable *on-dits*, but she drew the line at lightskirts. The worst calumny of that sort to pass her lips was that so and so was "keeping a woman."

The play seemed very long and dull. It was the Morgans' habit to have wine brought in at intermission, and as several friends stopped at their box, Devane was obliged to remain as well. Francesca went into the hallway to take a glass of wine and have a stroll. She noticed a few gentlemen gazing at her bosom, and remembered the patch. Lydia

Forsythe complimented her on it, and said jealously, "You have outdone yourself this time, Frankie! Honestly, I don't know how you come up with these clever ideas. And where does one buy patches in this day and age?" This question indicated an intention to follow the style, so Francesca left the patch where it was. She didn't even think to look around for Devane. She had forgotten all about him.

It took some doing to keep track of Mrs. Wilson's carriage in the mêlée after the play, but Devane's groom, from long practice, was quite a wizard in that respect. When the lady's carriage turned into Grosvenor Square, Devane's was only three carriages behind it. He frowned to see her carriage draw up in front of the perfectly respectable residence of Sir Giles and Lady Lister. Surely the chit was not bold enough to crash a polite party! No, the brown-haired gent escorting her must have some entrée to society. The Listers were not a couple whose party he would normally include in his rounds, but they were by no means on the fringes of society.

He watched as Mrs. Wilson was handed out by the brown-haired nonentity. He didn't recognize the other couple with her, but they looked respectable. By the time he entered the ballroom, Mrs. Wilson had not only been announced but had joined a set for a country dance. She heard the announcer call, "Lord Devane," and her head spun around. He stood behind an iron railing at the top of a shallow set of stairs, surveying the room as if he owned it. How arrogant he looked, how proud. She quickly turned her back to him, and was aware of a nervous dryness in her throat.

He couldn't possibly recognize her! She hadn't removed her mask at the Pantheon. He might see some resemblance, but when he heard her friends call her Frankie or Lady Camden, he would think he was mistaken. If he approached her, she would look right through him. What had she to worry about? *He* was the one who had behaved outrageously! Yet she felt guilty, and angry with herself for it. Why did he have to come here? She couldn't remember ever having attended the same party as him before, so they obviously traveled in different sets. He had come alone, without Lady Devane, if there was a Lady Devane. She was assailed by the awful idea that he had followed her.

When the music began, the motions of the dance distracted her to some extent. She looked around the room, wondering what set he had joined, but couldn't find him. Perhaps he was in the card parlor. She glanced toward the door, and there she saw him, hovering, looking directly at her through his raised quizzing glass. He looked like a vulture, all in black. She hastily averted her eyes and tried not to look at the doorway again. But her eyes were impossible to control. Again she looked, and again he was staring at her, wearing a sardonic smile now. She would not look again. He might mistake it for encouragement. Yet she was aware, without quite seeing him, that the black vulture never moved a muscle. At the end of the dance her nerves were stretched taut. She risked one last peek, and for a moment she breathed easy. He was gone.

Then she saw him working his way through the crowd straight toward her, and her blood chilled to ice. She turned to grab Selby's arm, but he had moved away. Her whole set were moving toward the refreshment parlor, but Francesca's legs seemed incapable of motion, and still he kept advancing. Within seconds he was at her side, bowing suavely.

"Good evening, Mrs. Wilson. We meet again." The words sounded like a challenge, and the sparkle in his eyes confirmed his mood.

There hardly seemed any point pretending, but she lifted her chin and said in a breathless voice that wouldn't fool a child, "I beg your pardon? Are you speaking to me, sir?"

He gave her a quizzing smile and glanced around the immediate area, which was bereft of other guests. "It looks like it, doesn't it? I am not flattered that you have forgotten me so soon, Mrs. Wilson. But then, I have been forewarned your memory is faulty. You forgot to return from the ladies' room the other evening."

"I can't imagine what you are talking about. I have never been inside the Pantheon in my life."

His smile stretched to a grin. "Why should you imagine I was speaking of the Pantheon?" he asked. A gasp of annoyance escaped her lips. "Come now, prevarication is pointless after that blunder, ma'am. The cat is out of the bag. You are you, and I am me. No hard feelings, but I do think you owe me an explanation."

"I don't know what you're talking about," she insisted, and turned bright pink.

"I take leave to inform you, Mrs. Wilson, that you are a wretched liar. Your explanation was highly unsatisfactory, but if you will bolster it up with a waltz, I shall accept it." The carved emerald on his finger glowed from the overhead chandeliers as his hand came out and fell on her arm. His grip felt like a manacle. Francesca looked up into his dark eyes, with that slash of brows lending him the air of a satyr.

Good God, she's frightened of me! Devane stared a moment, wondering if it was an act. But there was no air of coyness or teasing in her strained, pale face. His harsh features softened to a smile, and when he spoke, his voice was gentle, not the gentle silken menace she had heard before, but a warm gentleness. "I don't bite, you know. And I am considered a fair dancer. One dance, and if you aren't charmed by my nimble-footed Terpsichorean prowess, I'll let you go—most reluctantly."

He watched as she drew her bottom lip between her teeth, then slowly released it. "Well, one dance, then," she said, and smiled shyly.

"Unless you are charmed by my footwork, in which case I shall certainly be back to pester you for another waltz. You must not judge my performance by that free-for-all at the Pantheon."

"What makes you think it will be a waltz?"

"I have arranged it."

"You never left that wall. I saw you, staring at me, through your quizzing glass. I don't know why gentlemen employ them."

"The better to see you, my dear. I sent a footboy to the orchestra with a half crown. I begrudge no expense or trouble when I am—interested in a lady, you see."

She glanced at him from the corner of her eye and noticed Devane was peering at her patch. She was sorry she had not removed it. It seemed, suddenly, shoddy. Devane was not so stiff as she had feared, however, and she decided the easiest way out of this situation was to give him one dance and make a joke of the other evening. "A whole half crown. My, you are reckless, Lord Devane."

"Oh, you've cost me a good deal more than that already, and we haven't even—waltzed. I have had my spies out, trying to discover where I might find you."

"Very flattering, I'm sure. You make me feel like some sort of traitor."

"You are too harsh on yourself. *Deserter* would be my choice of word."

"Is Lady Devane aware of your lavish spending on another lady?" A tinge of ice coated her words, as it always did when she was reminded of David.

"No doubt she is frowning down on me from above."

Francesca glanced up to the platform, where new arrivals gathered. "Higher than that," he said. "I was saying, in my rather clumsy way, that my mother is dead. But what you were really asking was whether I am married. I'm not."

His being a bachelor lessened her ire somewhat. The music began, and he gathered her up in his arms. In this polite room he held her politely, their bodies an inch apart. His dancing lived up to his boast. He moved lightly and with grace and still managed to keep up a patter of conversation.

"Have you been in town long, Mrs. Wilson?"

"Going on three years, but this is only my second Season. Last year I was in mourning for my husband. He was killed in the Peninsula."

Devane examined this for credibility. Odd that she didn't wear a wedding ring, but she might have been married to an officer. Young gentlemen about to leave the country had made bad marriages before this, and their wives, wearing a thin coat of respectability, were permitted to loiter at the edge of society. If they were very pretty, as Mrs. Wilson was, they might advance a little deeper into the ton. Their aim was generally to make a second marriage that bettered their social standing. Mrs. Wilson's having inquired whether he was a bachelor suggested this was her aim. Her being at the Pantheon, on the other hand, suggested that she was not above a less formal liaison if there was something in it for her.

"It is odd I haven't seen you about before this," he said.

"It seems we attend different parties. I have heard of you, however."

"Nothing bad, I hope?"

"Mostly political things—you are a Whig, I think?"

"Guilty as charged. Your patch tells me we have that in common?"

She felt uncomfortable at the mention of that patch, and slid over it. "Oh, no, that is mere fashion. David—my husband's family are Tories. My papa has no interest in politics. He is a farmer." As Lord Devane was behaving like a gentleman, Francesca thought she ought to explain about calling herself Biddie Wilson.

He inclined his head and looked at her again with his disarming smile. "What a boor I am, discussing politics with a lady when we are waltzing."

"I expect that's a left-handed apology. I am the one who mentioned it first."

"I have heard of a left-handed compliment, but never a left-handed apology. You meant, of course, that I was chiding you under the guise of an apology. Guilty, as tacitly charged."

34

"That is twice you have told me what I meant. Do you read minds, Lord Devane?"

He peered down at her and smiled ingratiatingly. "I call it interpreting ladies' language. It is quite a foreign tongue to some of us gents. I, having spent some time in the territory, am conversant with the language. 'I look a quiz' means 'I have taken considerable trouble with my toilette and wish to be complimented.' 'You're early!' when said in a plaintive way means 'I am late.'"

"And when it is *not* said in a plaintive tone?"

"Why, then it means the lady is happy to see you."

"They say something is always lost in translation," she replied with a light laugh.

"You should do that more often, Mrs. Wilson— smile, I mean. You have a lovely smile." You look less like a lady of pleasure, he thought to himself. Yes, rather a sweet smile.

"Here is another speech for you to translate. I am not who you think I am."

"Not a Mrs., or not a Wilson?"

"Well," she said pensively, "not both. Really not either." The waltz ended. "I leave you with that little job of interpretation to think about."

He bowed while still holding her hand. "Don't worry. I didn't intend to forget you, Biddie."

She smiled and curtsied. "Thank you for an enjoyable dance, Lord Devane."

"Did you enjoy it?"

"You may feel free to interpret that, too," she teased, and disengaging her hand, she turned to leave.

Devane followed her from the floor. "I interpret

35

it to mean my dancing charmed you. Our bargain was that if it did, I had another dance."

"That is not how I interpreted it. Better take another ladies'-language lesson. Sorry." With a wave of her fingers, she hastened away.

Lady Lister was certainly charmed that the illustrious Devane honored her ball, and darted forth to nab him, and tour him about the room. "I see you have met Lady Camden," she said. "A charming girl."

Devane, for once, was shocked. "Lady Camden!"

"Yes, widow of Lord Camden, old Maundley's son, who was killed in the Peninsula. Not in the army precisely. He was sent over on some government commission and got in the way of a bullet. Francesca took it very hard, but she is recovering amazingly this year."

Was it possible Lady Lister was mistaken? "I thought she mentioned the name Wilson . . ."

"A Wilson before marriage. One of the Surrey Wilsons, Sir Gregory's daughter. Her mama is connected to the Beauforts. David was a wonderful catch for her, but then, she is so pretty. Come, you must meet the Landrys." She led him on, and while he bowed and smiled and made inconsequential chitchat, Devane assimilated the news that Biddie was a lady, and a widow. What he could not fathom was what a respectable, noble young widow had been doing at the Pantheon. There was a wild streak in the girl, obviously, or she would never have attracted that hell-raking young baron Camden. Wearing a patch where she wore it was a trifle fast, too. Such a lady might very well be interested in a discreet affair.

The nature of the affair would be somewhat

higher in tone then previously anticipated, and much more discreet. She would have to join his set, or he would have to join hers. Liaisons of the sort he had in mind were customarily carried out under the protective disguise of large house parties thrown by understanding hostesses. He was invited to two or three such parties in the near future.

When Francesca left Devane, she escaped to the refreshment parlor, where she joined Selby. "What had Devane to say?" he asked, worried. "Did he recognize you?"

"Yes, but I put him off. I don't think we need fear any bother from him. He seems quite nice, when you get to know him."

Mr. Caine assumed Devane had learned her true identity, and apologized for his error at the Pantheon. He joined her for the next set, and saw her safetly escorted for the one after that. Devane kept an eye on her but did not approach her. It was of prime importance now that the world not suspect anything between them. A lady's reputation must remain unsullied, especially when she was involved in an affair.

When he saw her stroll away from the ballroom a little later, however, he went after her and caught her up in the hallway. "Not leaving, I hope, Lady Camden?"

"Oh, you found out!" she said, and laughed.

"I cannot imagine why you chose to conceal such a respectable name."

"Because I was caught in such a scandalous situation, of course."

"Quite. The real question, however, is what you were doing there. Just out for an evening's hell-raising, I expect?"

She gave a weary sigh. "Well, one does get bored with all these formal dos."

He nodded. "I am attending an informal house party at the Duke of Tavistock's estate in Kent this weekend. Perhaps you would care to join me?"

She looked alarmed, even frightened. "Oh, no! I don't even know him."

"You know me."

Devane seemed to be two different people. There was the arrogant predator she met at the Pantheon, and the polite lord encountered earlier this evening. The gentleman she was with now was the arrogant predator. There was a certain gleam in his eye that slid too often to peer at her bosoms. That cursed patch! She raised her hand and covered her bodice.

"I am busy this weekend. Sorry."

"Next weekend, then, at Lady Jersey's place."

She gave up any pretense of politeness. "No!" she said sharply. "No, thank you," she modified when she saw his angry scowl. "I—I do not care for house parties."

"What entertainments *do* you care for, Lady Camden? I can suggest other outings."

"I wish you will not," she said crossly, and ran upstairs.

Devane stood in the hallway, looking up after her. He wore a pensive frown. Perhaps he was mistaken about Lady Camden, and she was not open to dalliance. Fair enough. He was not one to impose where he was not wanted.

But when he went home late that evening, he thought again of her angry reply to his different invitations. If she was not interested in an affair, one would have thought she would at least be interested in attaching an extremely eligible lord for a husband. She had no reason to know his advances were not honorable. The Pantheon had been a gaffe, but that was as much her doing as his. This evening he had been very proper in his dealings. So why had she scorned his advances? Damme, it was enough to make a man wonder if he was losing his grip.

Chapter Four

The next morning Lady Camden had an extremely unpleasant surprise. It was enough to knock all memory of Lord Devane out of her head. Her caller was Lord Maundley, who came once a month to pay his respects. He was an austere gentleman, so totally unlike his rakish son that it was hard to believe they were any relation at all. He was tall and ascetically thin, with gray hair pulled back from a high forehead. On his last visit he had queried her about the entailed jewelry David had given her. She had explained that David kept charge of it and had not given it to her when he left for Spain. It was arranged that Lord Maundley would check at David's bank to see if he had it put away in a safety box.

Francesca had heard no more about it, and assumed the jewelry was safe. It turned out Lord Maundley had recovered the case, but the star of the collection, a diamond necklace, was missing.

"I haven't seen it since David left," she said. "I

wore it only twice—for my presentation at court and the ball Lady Maundley gave before David left."

"I recall you were wearing it that evening." Maundley nodded. "Would you mind just taking a look among your things and see if it hasn't been misplaced?"

"But that was ages ago, Lord Maundley. I would have come across it before now. I recall perfectly David took it after the ball and put it in the case with the other pieces. I thought he had given the case to you before he left. He asked me if I wanted him to leave anything out to wear while he was away, but the Season was over, you know, and we thought he would be home in three months. I kept only the ring and brooch and ear pendants he gave me as a wedding gift. They were not entailed."

"Well, the diamond necklace is not in the case. What can have happened to it?" he demanded suspiciously. His piercing blue eyes almost suggested she had stolen it.

Francesca's color rose with her voice. "I haven't the faintest idea. I do not have the necklace. I haven't seen it since I handed it to David the night of the ball."

"That was two nights before he left for Spain. Are you sure he didn't give it back to you?"

"Positive. There was no reason to. We did not go out those two evenings. David had meetings at Whitehall the first evening, and the second, you and Lady Maundley dined with us. I did not wear the diamonds on either occasion."

"It is very vexing," he said, rubbing a sere white hand over his chin. "You must make a thorough search through all your things, and David's."

"I gave David's personal effects to Horton. I gave

41

away some of his clothes, but they were thoroughly searched before that."

"Whom did you give them to?" he demanded.

"To his cousin, George Devlin," she shot back. She had thought it rather ghoulish of George to want a dead man's clothing, even if it was elegant.

"We must instigate another search—his room, dresser, the attics. The necklace must be somewhere. It is not with the rest of the jewelry. I'll send my man over this afternoon to help you."

"That won't be necessary. My man will search," she said coldly.

But shortly after Maundley left, his valet arrived with instructions to search through all Lord Camden's rooms and cupboards. Francesca was incensed, but Mrs. Denver thought it might look as if they had something to conceal if they forbade it, so Munns was shown to David's room, and later to the attic, where he rummaged away at his pleasure.

The ladies did not go out that afternoon. They spent several hours in an utterly futile pawing through all their belongings. Later, they sat huddled together over their teacups, discussing the troublesome incident. "He probably gave it to one of his women," Francesca said bitterly. "I don't know what else could have happened to it. The night before he left, he said he was at Whitehall, but I doubt he was there till three in the morning. That is the hour he arrived home. And I, like a greenhorn, waiting up for him, pitying him." This disagreeable incident brought all the old pain back to the surface.

"Who was the woman?" Mrs. Denver asked.

"From what I have been able to find out, he had

42

broken off with Mrs. Ritchie the month before. I found a note in one of the jackets he wore at the time. It was signed *Rita*."

"No mention of a necklace?"

"No." She colored briskly at the contents of that note. *My dearest darling: You were wonderful last night,* followed by references of so intimate a nature that Francesca could hardly believe her eyes.

"Surely he wouldn't be fool enough to give entailed jewelry to a lightskirt," Mrs. Denver said.

"It would only have been a loan. He never dreamed he wouldn't come back."

"If that is what happened, someone must have seen it on her in the meanwhile. Perhaps Mr. Caine could look into it."

"She might have sold it when she heard David was dead," Francesca said uncertainly.

"You'll have to tell Maundley."

"Oh, dear! He doesn't know anything about David's women. It will break his heart—if he even believes me."

Mrs. Denver fretted and frowned, then said, "Did the government send back his things from Spain? I was thinking, he might have taken it with him."

"Yes, for what purpose you can well imagine! It wasn't returned with his personal effects. If he gave it to a senorita, it is lost for good."

At four o'clock Munns appeared at the doorway and announced that he had not found the necklace. "I shall report to Lord Maundley," he said grandly, and left.

That evening Lord Devane scoured London in vain for a glimpse of Lady Camden. She was at home, discussing the matter with Selby Caine and her aunt. Mr. Caine was in his element, with a potential tragedy in the making.

"I've told you often enough no good would come of this, Fran. Long threatening comes at last. A lady called Rita, you say? No idea of the last name?"

"None," Francesca replied glumly.

"I hardly know where to begin. I have no connection with ladies of that sort. Riffraff, leading lives of chaos and degradation. I stay well away from them. Perhaps John Irwin can give me a lead," he said, naming a friend who flew somewhat higher than himself. "He's usually to be found at Brooke's of an evening. At least it keeps him away from the muslin company. I'll drop around and see if he has any ideas."

Mr. Irwin, a dapper gentleman with twinkling blue eyes and a lively sense of the ridiculous, came to call with Caine the next afternoon. Unlike Mr. Caine, Mr. Irwin fancied himself up to all the rigs. He poke cant as fluently as a scholar spoke Latin, and was eager to put himself at Lady Camden's disposal.

"Can you describe the necklace for me, Lady Camden?" he asked.

"A chain of small stones that hung just below the collarbone, with a rather ugly crown-shaped piece of larger diamonds pendant at the front. Oh, and the clasp at the back had some small rubies."

"That is pretty distinctive. It shouldn't be hard to recognize."

"You haven't seen it about?" Mrs. Denver asked.

"The lady would have squirreled it away once she heard of Camden's death."

"Or sold it," Mr. Caine added dampeningly.

"I shouldn't think so. The jewelers are familiar with the valuable pieces of entailed jewelry. She might have placed it with a lock if she was desperate for money. Rum quids for them. The stalling kens wouldn't give her a tenth of what it was worth, though."

Mrs. Denver knew her hearing was on the decline and touched her ear. "I beg your pardon, Mr. Irwin. I didn't quite catch that."

"She might have taken it to Stop Hole Abbey."

"Where is that?"

He gave a knowing little laugh. "You must pardon my speaking cant, ma'am. The lady might have placed it with a receiver of stolen goods is what I mean. He would pay her a small fraction of what it is worth, pull the thing apart, and sell the stones separately."

"Then we'll *never* recover it!" Francesca wailed.

"I've warned you often enough you were skating on thin ice," Mr. Caine said glumly. His swaying had assumed the speed of a ladies' fan as he waved to and fro.

"For goodness' sake, sit down, Selby," Francesca said curtly.

Mr. Irwin continued his discourse undismayed. "Stop Hole Abbey would be a lady's last resort. Unless she is flat in the stirrups, I daresay she's just sitting on it, a nest egg for her old age. Never fear, ladies, we'll whiddle the whole scrap for you. I'll take a run down to Stop Hole Abbey and play the sly boots. If the necklace was placed on the table, I'll soon know about it. Can you come up with the spankers to redeem it if the lock happened to hold on to it?"

"Can you not speak English, John?" Selby said.

"Do you mean money to buy it back?" Francesca asked Irwin.

"Precisely."

"How much would it cost?" Mrs. Denver asked fearfully.

"I'll let you know."

"I don't see why *I* should pay!" Francesca objected.

"No more you should," Irwin agreed. "Hit Maundley up for it."

"Oh, but he doesn't know about my husband's affairs."

"He must keep his ears waxed. Whole town knows. But before I visit the locks, I'll speak to a couple of fellows who know all the muslin company and see if I can learn who this Rita is. I'll have a word with Dawson, Lord Etherington, Devane."

"No!" Lady Camden exclaimed loudly, and won the attention of the whole group. "I would prefer not to involve Devane in this affair."

"Whyever not?" Irwin asked, intrigued. Was there something afoot here he hadn't heard about?

"We think he may be interested in Lady Camden," Caine explained vaguely. "I told her he flew too high."

Irwin's eyebrows rose an inch. "I shouldn't think that is anything to keep under the covers. Extremely eligible. The premier parti for several Seasons now."

"He is not interested in me, and I do not wish to involve him," Lady Camden said very firmly.

"Just as you wish, madam. You have no objection to my speaking discreetly to Dawson and Lord Etherington?"

"None in the world."

"I shall keep my peepers open as well. Cyprian's ball is coming up. Our mysterious Rita might venture to wear it there, among her own set. You may be sure it is no secret she has the thing."

Mr. Irwin soon left and went eagerly about the business of making inqueries. Mr. Caine remained behind to read the ladies a lecture.

"Are you sure that young gentleman's discretion is to be counted on?" Mrs. Denver asked.

Mr. Selby was coerced into taking a seat, and gave his pronouncement. "His heart is in the right place. Whether he can hold his tongue, there is no saying, but something had to be done. I haven't many acquaintances who are likely to know any lightskirts. If the thing is not found, there will be rumors aplenty. Better the blame be directed to the proper source than to Fran. What remains of her reputation would be in utter ruin."

"If worst comes to worst, you'll just have to tell Maundley the truth," Mrs. Denver said, and drew a weary sigh.

Francesca pondered this. The old pain and sorrow seemed new again. They sat like a leaden boulder on her heart. David's awful behavior would seem even worse to his strict parents. Why subject an old man and his invalid wife to that agony if it could possibly be avoided? She would gladly sacrifice her wedding jewelry to buy the necklace back if that was the only way to conceal the story. Of course her gift from David wouldn't begin to cover the cost. "I hope it doesn't come to that," she said.

"Would you like to go out this evening and forget your troubles for an hour or two, Fran?" Selby asked. He felt sorry for her. Her shoulders sagged, and her face was strained with worry.

She looked up, surprised at this suggestion from such an unlikely source as Mr. Caine. "Not tonight, thank you, Selby. I don't feel up to it."

"I meant only a concert of antique music. I find the old composers settle my nerves. But just as you wish," he replied, trying to conceal his relief. "You wouldn't be eager to go out at this time." He left soon afterward.

With no troublesome lady to protect, Selby spent his evening at Brooke's Club, where he encountered Mr. Irwin. They hailed each other, and went to a table set apart from the others for private conversation.

"Any luck, John?" Selby asked eagerly.

"Did you ever notice how names go in Season?" was Mr. Irwin's seemingly irrelevant reply. "I mean, you take the turn of the century. A hundred chits called Georgiana after the Duchess of Devonshire. There are dozens of Charlottes and Carolines after the royal family, and Arabella caught on for some reason. You don't hear so often of a Mary or an Anne nowadays."

"But have you heard of a Rita?" Selby asked, to recall his friend to the problem at hand.

"That's just what I'm getting at. Rita is the name for lightskirts this Season. They all change their names, you know."

"Well they might, the shameful creatures. But are you saying they are all called Rita? Is it a generic thing, like calling our grooms John?"

"No, it is merely a fashion. Daresay they think Rita has a touch of foreign allure. There is Rita Delaney, and Rita Morrow, and Marguerita Sullivan—but her *intimes* call her Rita."

"Any reason to think Camden was trifling with any of them?"

"Not with Delaney. She was brought over from the ould sod by Lord Munster, and is more or less faithful to him. Morrow—now, there is a possibility, and Sullivan as well. They change partners a fair bit. I have a meeting with Morrow tomorrow. Is that a pun? No, of course not. What an ass I am. I shan't just blurt out 'Have you got Lady Camden's diamond necklace?' but I shall nose around. Marguerita Sullivan will be harder to approach. She's under old Sir Percy's protection. He is jealous as a sultan. He'd run his rusty sword through anyone he caught sniffing around her. Mind you, he might miss. He's blind in one eye and don't see too well out of the other."

"Have you been to Stop Hole Abbey?"

"One does not go to Stop Hole Abbey in daylight, my good fellow. One approaches under cover of darkness. Arrangements have to be made. I'm meeting a scapegallows at midnight. He's on the star lag." Mr. Caine looked a question at him. "Don't you know *anything*, Caine? The fellow busts windows and runs off with the loot. Care to come along?"

"Only if I am needed," Mr. Caine said reluctantly.

"Not necessary. Two ears are as good as four. I just thought a sparkish fellow like you might enjoy the spree."

Mr. Caine was flattered to be called a sparkish fellow, but he always preferred to avoid anything smelling of a spree. Francesca's sprees were more than enough excitement for him. "Not if I can help it, thank you."

"What the deuce is a fellow like you doing running around with the infamous Frankie Devlin if you ain't up to all the rigs? I mean, she's not exactly a prude, is she?"

"Oh, she is troubled, poor girl. To tell the truth, I am getting tired of pulling her chestnuts from the fire. She is too frivolous for my taste. Leading men on—but there is no vice in her after all. Her innocence leads her astray. Pray forget I said a word against her. I'll call on you tomorrow morning if you're free?"

"Not before noon, if you please. I never rise or drink before the sun is at its zenith."

Mr. Caine thanked his friend and left. He had little notion how he might help find the necklace, but knew lightskirts hung out at the Pantheon, and went there, to squint at all the ladies' throats, in hopes of seeing the crown-shaped pendant. He fancied that what he saw was mostly strass glass, and went home at midnight, thinking of Mr. Irwin on his way to meet with criminals and ruffians.

He would not desert Francesca in her hour of need, but after this was over, he meant to go back home to Surrey. She was not his problem after all, and he was tired of London.

Chapter Five

Lord Devane, seated at a table in the middle of the room, noticed when Caine left, and at the end of his game he strolled nonchalantly toward Mr. Irwin. He knew the man to nod to, but couldn't put a name to him. He had also recognized the brown-haired gent with him as a friend of Lady Camden's. "Is this seat free?" he asked in a casual manner.

"Ah, Lord Devane! Sit thee down, I pray. Delighted for some cheerful company. Have a glass of brandy." Irwin waved for a fresh glass, and poured his guest a shot.

"Was your friend, the man who just left, not cheerful company?" Devane inquired blandly.

"Selby Caine cheerful? Ho, is a martyr cheerful? Is Job cheerful? I've never seen Caine smile in my life, though he's a sound chap."

"What troubles him?"

"The world troubles him, milord. He could find mischief lurking in an essay by Hannah More. He would prefer to live in a monastery or a hermit's

51

cave, I fancy. How he ever got mixed up with Lady Camden—"

"Ah, that would be the young lady I've seen him about with. A striking brunette?" Mr. Irwin nodded. "Lovely girl, Lady Camden. I have met her once or twice."

"Yes, but lovely is as lovely does, to coin a not very original phrase. A bit of a cutup, young Frankie Devlin."

"Is that what folks call her, Frankie?"

"She used to be called Francesca, Fran for short, but when Camden stuck his fork in the wall, she turned into a hellion and changed her name to Frankie. Old Caine is fed up with her pranks. Damme! He asked me not to say so. Delete it from your memory, Lord Devane."

"Consider it deleted, but just *entre nous*"—he inclined his head forward in a man-to-man way that was irresistible to Irwin, especially when coming from the great Devane—"the lady is a bit of a dasher, eh?"

"Well, she ain't a Bath Miss, that much at least I can say without shocking even Mr. Caine. She gave young Stanby pretty short shrift just last week. In short, milord, a gazetted flirt. But Caine tells me there is no vice in her. She lets it all out—ha-ha!"

Devane did not wish to be too obvious, and let the topic rest a moment. Irwin immediately broached the subject of names, to be precise, the name Rita. "Very popular with the muslin company this Season. You must have noticed—a man like you."

"I can't say it had occurred to me. I rather thought Marie held sway this year."

"It's as I said to Caine. The touch of French—they think it glamorous." Irwin filled his own glass and topped off Lord Devane's.

"Speaking of exotic names—Francesca, that would be Italian, would it not?" Devane said, to return to his preferred subject.

"Sounds like it. Where the Wilsons picked up an Italian name is a mystery to me. They're as English as cod."

"Do you know Lady Camden well?"

Irwin's smile was becoming a trifle unsteady. "She is a new acquaintance, but I shall know her better after I have—that is—er, soon."

"Ah." The single syllable was fraught with conspiratorial, gentlemanly understanding.

Irwin put his finger aside his nose and tapped. "Diamonds," he said, nodding sagely.

"The lady has a fondness for diamonds, you mean?"

"Haven't all ladies?" Irwin asked cagily.

"They do seem to hold universal appeal."

"Would you care for a hand of cards, Devane?" Mr. Irwin asked.

"Delighted."

"What is the hour?" Irwin drew out his watch. "No, by gad, I must be off to Stop Hole Abbey for the diamonds. I'm visiting St. Peter's son—the gents with fish hooks for fingers. Another time, Devane. Delightful chatting to you." He rose, bowed two or three times, and left at an unsteady gait. Devane heard someone call him "Irwin" as he left.

Devane sat on alone, thinking. He had already heard rumors that Lady Camden was making a name for herself. The worst he had learned was that she was a flirt. That she was about to receive a

53

diamond necklace from Irwin suggested her flirtation was stepping up to more advanced dalliance. And Irwin, the fool, was obtaining his bribe at Stop Hole Abbey. He might count himself fortunate if he didn't end up in Newgate for buying stolen goods.

Devane did not by any means consider himself his brother's keeper. His mind soon wandered off in a quite different direction. He had been to half a dozen routs and assemblies looking for Francesca. His mind played with the name. Its soft syllables suited her; Frankie, on the other hand, had a harsh, rowdy sound to it. He would call her Francesca when she was under his protection. But meanwhile, where was she hiding herself? Was the wench purposely staying away to whet his appetite?

She had declined an invitation to two unexceptionable house parties, but apparently welcomed a set of diamonds from a Mr. Irwin, of no particular consequence. She was either mad, or considered herself uncommonly clever. Perhaps she was using Irwin to make him jealous? He soon concluded this was her strategy, and decided two could play at that game. He would be seen around with the Season's prettiest lightskirt. Marie Mondale, perhaps? He would escort her to Covent Garden the following evening. If Lady Camden did not attend, she would at least hear of it. Let her see a lady could play too hard to get.

The next morning Mr. Caine and Mr. Irwin came to call at Half Moon Street. "The diamonds were never sold at Stop Hole Abbey," Mr. Irwin announced. "Whoever has them, she's sitting on them, as I said. I haven't been able to discover who this Rita is that Camden was seeing, but I am seeing Rita Morrow as soon as I leave you. There is no guarantee she is the right Rita. There are half a dozen Ritas this Season. I shall return and let you know what develops, Lady Camden."

"You are very kind, Mr. Irwin," she said, and smiled her appreciation. "I am sorry to put you to so much bother."

"Why, it is pure pleasure for me, aiding a lady in distress."

"Still, it is a great deal of bother."

"If you wish to reward me, drive out with me when I return. Perhaps we will think of some other course to follow to retrieve the necklace."

"I will be happy to."

Mr. Caine stood in the corner, swaying and worrying while this conversation went forth. At its end, he left with Irwin, and Mrs. Denver said. "Mr. Irwin has an eye for you, Fran. You must not encourage him unless—"

"Set up a flirtation with him, you mean? No, I never would when he is being so nice and helpful."

"Why, you sound as though you run around only with gentlemen you dislike!"

Francesca laughed this absurd idea away, but when she was alone later, she remembered it and wondered. It was true, her requirements for flirts were two; first, that they were manageable, for she did not intend to let herself be taken advantage of. The other was that she knew in advance she could never truly care for them. If they had a touch of David's glib insincerity, so much the better. She could punish him through them. Was that what she had been doing?

She soon forgot Mr. Irwin. He was nothing like David. It was Lord Devane who she thought of longer. Yes, there was certainly something of David in that gentleman's easy advances, but he failed her other criterion. He was not a safe man to trifle with. She had not heard from him since he learned she was a fine lady, however, and she considered that the end of the matter.

Her real concern was the diamond necklace, and that was what brought the worried frown to her brow. Lord Maundley had sent a curt note. "You were the last person seen to have the diamonds. I consider them your responsibility. If they are not found, then I will expect restitution to be made." It was as good as a threat. He obviously thought she had them.

Lunch was a desultory meal. Neither Mrs. Denver nor Francesca ate much. "I hope Mr. Irwin learns something from that Rita woman," Francesca said.

"He couldn't ask her on their first meeting. It will take a few outings to soften her up," Mrs. Denver replied.

"I wonder how soon Maundley will act."

"That is all a bluff. What can he do, when all is said and done?"

"Hire a lawyer to harass me, I suppose."

"You must tell the lawyer what happened to the necklace."

"He would be sure to tell Maundley. I do dislike to cause them anxiety, especially Lady Maundley. She was so fond of David. It would break her heart."

"Better her heart than your reputation."

Francesca put her face in her hands and emitted a strangled moan. "As if David was not thorn enough in my side when he was alive, now he puts me through this hell." She rose from the table and went upstairs.

Mrs. Denver suspected she was having a good cry, and left her alone. When Francesca came down, there was no sign of tears. She was smiling wanly, and spoke hopefully of Mr. Irwin's learning something to help them. When that gentleman called, she was looking very pretty in her new yellow straw bonnet and light pelisse. "Any luck with Rita Morrow, Mr. Irwin?" she asked before leaving, for Mrs. Denver would not want to be kept in the dark on this point till after the drive.

He shook his head. "Nothing firm, I fear."

They drove to Hyde Park, oblivious to the blue skies, the stately parade of trees, and the soft breezes of spring. Mr. Irwin tried to assuage her fears by speaking hopefully of other schemes to assist her. He was planning to tour the jewelry shops in town, inquiring for the necklace. "No jeweler would buy it, but that is not to say they have not been offered it. If they have, perhaps I can get a lead on who offered it for sale."

"Would they not have notified Lord Maundley if they recognized it as a family heirloom?" she asked.

"They ought to have, of course, but if the hopeful seller was a good customer, they might have desisted."

"Then they will not likely tell *you*, will they, Mr. Irwin?"

This sort of common sense had no place on a lady's tongue, in Mr. Irwin's opinion. "There are ways of rattling their chains," he said curtly.

She was impressed with his surly manner as she took it for a taste of how he would deal with unscrupulous jewelry salesmen. "You mean—threats?" she asked, her eyes brimming with admiration.

This hadn't occurred to him, but he seized the

idea as his own and nodded bravely. "I shall also keep my eyes open on any occasion when I am likely to run into members of the muslin company. Not that I would meet them by choice, but they are seen about everywhere nowadays." His frown suggested he was every bit as much against this deterioration of society as even Mr. Caine could wish.

"I doubt the woman would wear it in public."

"A year has passed, and no alarm has been raised. She may be gaining confidence that she's pulled it off. It's worth a thought. Tonight at Covent Garden, for instance, the cream of the muslin company will attend the opening of Kemble's *Bluebeard*. It is to be a great lavish thing, with elephants and sixteen horses. You will be attending, of course?"

"No," Francesca said listlessly. "Till this business is settled, I haven't the heart for it."

He decided the lady needed cheering, and began to rally her spirits at once. "What, give in to a thieving lightskirt? Let a female like that drive you into hiding? Bosh. You shall come to Covent Garden with me this evening. We shall ignore the stage and train our glasses on every neck that sparkles. Come along, do, Lady Camden."

"I'm not sure I am up to it."

"Why, you will give Maundley the notion you take his threat seriously. He whiddles beef and you brush. It looks like capitulation on your part if you withdraw from the fray. He'll think you're guilty. Withdrawal will certainly be taken as a sign of weakness at least. You must let him see you don't give a tinker's curse for his ranting."

"I wouldn't want him to think I am afraid," she said thoughtfully.

"Excellent, then I shall take you to Covent Garden this evening. We'll escape that croaker of a Caine if we can. We shall have a merry old time, I promise you, and a tidy dinner later at the Clarendon, with a few select friends."

"Perhaps I should go." She agreed with very little enthusiasm for the project.

As Mr. Irwin's chaise left the park, it passed a dashing black carriage with a lozenge on the door. It was the spanking team of bays that drew Mr. Irwin's attention, but it was the gentleman who nodded from the window who made Francesca's breath catch in her throat. It was Lord Devane, and he had a beautiful woman with him. He nodded with cool politeness as they passed.

"That was Lord Devane," she mentioned to Mr. Irwin. "Did you recognize the lady with him? She was a redhead—very lovely."

"I just caught a glimpse, but it looked like Marie Mondale, one of this Season's belles."

"Marie Mondale? I don't recognize the name. . . ."

"No more you would, my dear. She ain't precisely a lady, if you catch my meaning. It is as I said, one sees them everywhere."

Francesca understood him perfectly. She felt a burning annoyance at Devane's blatant parading of a lightskirt in a polite park. That was the sort of thing David would have done. They were cut from the same bolt. She hardly listened as Mr. Irwin praised the bays.

Lord Devane had no business publicly engaging a mistress when he was interested in herself, Francesca thought. He had implied he was interested at the ball the other evening. He had been running after her as hard as he could, bribing the musicians

59

to play a waltz and trying to get her to stand up with him a second time. That augured a strong interest—but the minute her back was turned, he was out with lightskirts.

"Let us go home," she said angrily.

Mr. Irwin didn't argue. He was finding the widow very attractive and hoped to win her favor by recovering her necklace. He would run around to Rundell and Bridges and the other good jewelry shops to make inquiries. Not that they'd tell him if they had seen it, but they might have a sketch of the thing, as they had of the country's more prized heirlooms. At least he would know what he was looking for.

Mrs. Denver was surprised to hear that Francesca was going out that evening, but when the reason was explained, she nodded her agreement. She hoped that Mr. Irwin would succeed, and become a hero, at least long enough for Francesca to accept an offer from him. She saw marriage as the only possible solution to her charge's problem.

Chapter Six

Lady Camden went to the theater with no notion of enjoying herself or even of giving more than a passing glance at the play. It proved impossible to entirely ignore a stage where an extravagant piece featuring an elephant and sixteen horses was in progress, however. She had never seen a live elephant before, and gaped in awe like the rest of the audience. *Bluebeard* was a great popular success and proved so distracting that it was only at the intermissions that Francesca remembered to scan the lightskirts' throats for her diamonds.

Lord Devane was more debonair. He had seen an elephant before, and while the throng gasped at the menagerie onstage, he lifted his glasses and scrutinized the boxes. Yes, there she was, and with her Mr. Irwin and Mr. Caine. Rather odd, that. He lowered his glasses to her creamy throat, and saw, sitting against her pale skin, not a diamond necklace, but a somewhat insignificant strand of pearls. Her late husband could not have left her well provided for, or she would be wearing diamonds. Had Mr.

Irwin failed to procure her a set at Stop Hole Abbey? He lowered his glasses even farther, to look for the patch. It was missing, though he had seen patches on a few other ladies after the Incomparable introduced the notion.

He regarded her a long time, taking in every feature of her face, and every item of her apparel. The Incomparable was introducing no new fashion this evening. Her toilette was unexceptionable, but it lacked her usual fliar. He noticed the girlish smile hovering about her lips as she gazed in rapture at the stage. There was still something of the girl in her. He rather liked that. A little town bronze was all well and good, but he didn't want a jaded sophisticate.

Mr. Irwin had chosen his party with care to provide no competition for Lady Camden's attention. His sister, a flat, had requested that he ask Mr. Caine as her escort. Finding escorts for Lavinia was always a problem, and he had acquiesced to having Job along. Mr. Caine's sole comment on the first act was that the play must have cost a great deal of money to produce. Even a full house could not possibly cover the cost. The third couple were married, a Mr. Grant and his wife, who were respectable rather than *tonnish*.

When the curtain closed for the first intermission, Irwin leaned over to Lady Camden and said, "Now is our chance to check the ladies for the glass. You take the left side of the theater, I'll take the right. Don't waste time on anything but the boxes."

She understood this to mean that David's flirts were too high to sit anywhere but in a box. There was a great commotion of people leaving for a stroll in the hall, to greet their friends and exercise their legs after a long sit. It was difficult to know where to begin looking. Jewelry glittered everywhere in the flickering lights of the chandeliers. The gemstones—diamonds, sapphires, and rubies—came in combinations, and they all glowed, so it was difficult to distinguish diamonds at a distance.

Francesca found the most efficacious way was to glance first at the lady's face, and if she recognized it as belonging to a respectable lady, she moved her glasses along. There was no point thinking Lady Jersey or Lady Castlereagh would be wearing stolen jewelry. To her consternation, she soon realized that half the women present were not ladies, which left a great many necklaces to be examined.

From her box on the right side of the hall, she moved her glasses over the boxes on the left. One box caught her particular attention. It held three bucks and three of the loveliest young women she had ever seen, none of whom she recognized at first glance. She trained her glasses to examine their jewelry. One, a blonde, was wearing sapphires. A brunette wore pearls, and the third, a redhead, wore diamonds. A quick glimpse revealed some similarity to her necklace. She adjusted her glasses for a sharper look. No, they were similar, but far from identical.

As she was looking, a hand appeared on the lady's white shoulder. The fingers moved, giving the shoulder an intimate squeeze, and on the small finger sat a carved emerald. A spontaneous gasp escaped her lips, and she moved the glasses to the man's face. There, looking close enough to touch, was Lord Devane. His lips moved in some tender endearment, then widened in a smile. Just so had he smiled at her at the ball. He hadn't seen her.

He inclined his head closer to the redhead. Francesca adjusted her focus for a good study of the lady's face, and recognized the woman from Devane's carriage. Marie Mondale, Mr. Irwin had called her. Francesca admitted that he looked extremely attractive, his hair so dark and his face so rugged. The woman opened her lips, revealing perfect white teeth, and laughed provocatively up at him. Devane inclined his head and touched his lips to her naked shoulder. The lady rose, and they left the box arm in arm.

Francesca moved her glasses away hastily before he saw her. Not that he appeared interested in anything but the woman he was with! She felt a raging inside that she hadn't felt since her first knowledge of David's perfidy. Men were all alike! Bad enough they had their unsavory affairs, but to be parading their women in front of respectable people! Her chest heaved in vexation.

She jumped in surprise when Mr. Irwin reached out and touched her shoulder. "Nothing on this side. Did you have any luck?"

"No."

"Shall we go out for a glass of wine?"

"I would rather remain here, thank you. One meets such unsavory types wandering the halls." Types like Devane, and his mistress.

"I'll bring you a glass, shall I?"

"Thank you, if you will be so kind."

Mr. Caine and Miss Irwin had left, but the Grants remained behind to keep Lady Camden company. Their chatter was all about the play. "I wouldn't have missed it for a wilderness of monkeys," Mrs. Grant said.

Mr. Grant fancied he knew what the more demanding critics would think. "It is good enough entertainment, but one can hardly call it a play," he objected. "Poor Kemble owes the theater proprietors a fortune, and is reduced to such 'draws' as this. We shan't see *Macbeth* or *Lear* for many a long month, I fear."

"That's good, then," his wife said bluntly. "Did you see the elephant butt that actor with his trunk? I thought he would come tumbling off the stage. Isn't it marvelous, Lady Camden?"

"Lovely."

The Grants' excited chatter concealed any lack of enthusiasm on Francesca's part. She would never hear the word *elephant* again without seeing that white shoulder with the ringed hand gripping it. The lips touching that white shoulder . . . A shiver ran across her scalp. She could almost feel those lips caressing her own flesh. Horrid, wanton man. Such intimate pleasures should be restricted to the boudoir—and to marriage.

Mr. Irwin returned with the wine, and the conversation continued to revolve around the play. "I fear it signals the end of drama as we know it" was Mr. Caine's opinion. "It is fatally easy for the public taste to be degraded, but to raise it again—it is all but impossible. What will Kemble show us next year? Wild tigers, monkeys? It don't bear thinking about."

At the last intermission Mr. Irwin again suggested a stroll, and again Lady Camden declined, adding, "You go ahead, Mr. Irwin."

"But I cannot leave you alone. The others have left."

There was a commotion at the door of their box, and a young couple entered. It was Sir Bedford and

Lady Harcourt, friends of Francesca's. Mr. Irwin could then leave with honor.

"We spotted you across the hall and had to drop in." Lady Harcourt smiled. "Delicious play, is it not?"

"Very amusing, and so unusual," Francesca replied. "I have never seen an elephant before."

They chatted for two or three minutes. The Harcourts wished to visit other friends as well but did not like to leave Francesca alone. When the door opened and another caller entered, they hastily took their leave. Francesca looked into the shadows to see who was calling and saw Lord Devane. Her heart began hammering. She thought of running out after the Harcourts, but it was too late. They were gone.

Devane's severe face was wearing a smile as it emerged from the shadows into the front of the box. "Good evening, Lady Camden. Aren't I fortunate to find you alone? I had not looked for such luck as that."

Her lips thinned, her nostrils pinched, and her voice was frosty. "Good evening, Lord Devane."

"You must be the only lady in the house who is not smiling at this delightful performance," he said, tilting his head playfully to examine her. Oh, yes, she had seen him with Marie, right enough. Why else would she be looking daggers at him? Excellent!

"Do you think so? I doubt your partner is smiling, to see you desert her at the intermission."

"I did not leave her alone. Marie is with friends."

"She is not with the gentleman who brought her."

66

"Nor are you. It is remiss of Mr. Irwin to leave you alone."

"I was not alone! I was with my friends, till you chased them away."

"I was under the impression they were just leaving. May I?" He put his hand on the back of the chair next to her, and sat down without waiting for permission. Obviously he could not leave her alone. "What has put you in such a pucker, ma'am? Am I about to hear how Kemble has set drama back a hundred years?"

"It's not exactly Shakespeare, is it?"

"For small mercies, let us be thankful. The best Shakespeare could do for us was a bear—in *The Winter's Tale*."

"If you want to see wild animals, you should go to the Exeter Exchange," she snipped, pulling her shawl about her shoulders.

"One monkey is much like another, and one tires of that hippopotamus. I am always willing to settle for a wildcat," he added with a bold grin as his eyes moved over her face, lingering a moment on her eyes, her nose, and, lastly, her lips.

"If you expect to see me bare my claws in public, you will be disappointed. Some things ought to be done in private," she said, glaring.

"That is easily arranged."

"Then might I suggest you take her to your pied-à-terre on the Chelsea Road and arrange it, sir? We came to see the play onstage, not in the boxes."

"You have obviously been casting your glasses in the wrong direction, ma'am. My box is some yards away from the stage." He glanced across the hall to it. "Fairly dark, too. I am flattered that you singled it out for your attentions. Had I known, I would have behaved more discreetly."

"I doubt that."

"There's still one act to go. You will observe— through your glasses—that I behave with the utmost discretion. Mind you, I cannot speak for my partner. Marie is hot-blooded."

Francesca's own blood was in some danger of boiling, but her face looked frozen. She was happy for an interruption, yet not entirely happy either. She enjoyed this verbal jousting with Lord Devane. If only she could get the better of him! "Ah, here is Mr. Irwin, returned with wine. I suggest you return to Marie before her blood reaches the boil. Good evening, sir. So kind of you to keep me company."

"I fear I speak the simple truth when I say the pleasure was all mine, madam." He bowed gracefully, nodded to Mr. Irwin, and left.

"What the devil was Devane doing here?" Mr. Irwin asked. His concern was for the competition this illustrious gentleman presented. He could see, however, that Lady Camden was displeased with the visit.

"He stopped by to say good evening."

"I had the impression, last evening, that he didn't know you that well."

Lady Camden's eyes flew to his in chagrin. "What do you mean, last evening? Was he asking about me?"

"Just a word in passing. We happened to meet at Brooke's Club. He had seen me with Caine—your name came up somehow or other. He mentioned the lovely lady he had seen with Mr. Caine—something of the sort. I remember you particularly discouraged me from asking his help."

"We met only a few days ago. I did not want you to pester a mere acquaintance. What did he say about me?"

"Now, it is nothing to get in a pucker over, my dear. He scarcely mentioned your name, I promise you. You need not fear him. He is no prude, but he would never dishonor a lady of unsullied reputation. He has lightskirts enough without ruining ladies. Well, he is a bachelor after all, and a highly eligible one, too. He owns St. Alban's Abbey and an estate in Somerset, to say nothing of his hunting box and London mansion."

Francesca was gratified to hear she had drawn the attention of such a wealthy gentleman, and let the matter drop.

"Who is he with this evening, I wonder?" Mr. Irwin asked. Francesca directed him to the proper box but was careful not to look within a right angle of it herself for the remainder of the evening. She suspected Lord Devane might be casting an occasional glance at her, however, and began flirting discreetly with Mr. Irwin.

Lord Devane did indeed take an occasional glance, no more. He was too clever, and too proud, to make a cake of himself. He divined her trick, and knew he had caught her interest. When the play was over, their two parties went to separate hotels to dine, and they did not see each other again that evening. Mrs. Denver had retired by the time Francesca got home, so she went directly to bed.

The evening had been a dead loss so far as finding the necklace was concerned, but Lady Camden was by no means in the mopes. She was young enough to be elated at having caught the interest of the Season's most eligible bachelor. Her first fear of not being able to handle him diminished when Mr. Irwin assured her his reputation was good. Perhaps she would flirt with him a little next time they met. But she would never marry someone like him. One David in a lifetime was more than enough.

Chapter Seven

Mrs. Denver was happy to see her charge in good spirits the next morning. "Any luck at the theater?" she asked eagerly.

"No sign of the necklace, but the play was very interesting. They had a live elephant onstage, Mrs. Denver. You really must go to see it."

"It sounds dangerous. What if it got loose?"

"It didn't. Mr. Irwin is visiting the jewelers' shops this morning to try to get a lead on the necklace."

"How kind of him." Mr. Irwin appeared to be gaining favor. She must learn more about him from Mr. Caine before the thing became serious. "Are you driving out with him later?" she asked.

"No. I shall stay home today. Truth to tell, I am tired of racketing around town."

"You have been trotting pretty hard," Mrs. Denver agreed, and hid her astonishment as well as she could. This didn't look like infatuation. Mrs. Denver felt no invitation had been extended, but when—if—it was, Fran would no doubt accept. To her surprise, Francesca did nothing of the sort. Mr. Irwin did stop by and invite her out, but she refused two or three times, till at last he accepted her decision.

"You ought not to have refused just because he failed to find out anything from the jewelers, Fran," Mrs. Denver admonished Frankie. "The man is doing his best. He spent his entire morning working for you."

"Oh, was I rude?" she asked. "I shall drive out the next time he calls."

"Why did you not go today?"

"I don't feel like going out, with this necklace business hanging over my head," Francesca replied, and hoped her aunt would not inquire further. To herself she admitted that what kept her home was the possibility that Lord Devane might call. He had not asked for permission to do so, but then, he was of that class that hardly required permission. A call from Lord Devane was considered an honor.

The hour from two to three dragged by, and Francesca was obliged to pretend satisfaction with her dull day. She leafed desultorily through fashion magazines but could not settle down to anything more demanding. At three on the dot the knocker sounded, and she leapt in her chair. "Who can that be?"

"Probably Mr. Caine," Mrs. Denver said. She did not recognize Lord Devane's deep voice, but Francesca did, and assumed a bored expression, but with a telltale glitter in her eyes.

Francesca overcame all her reluctance to leave the house, and sent off for her bonnet and pelisse as soon as Devane mentioned a drive in the park. Mrs. Denver could only stare in surprised dismay. He was hardly the sort Fran usually had her harmless little flings with. An acknowledged man-about-town—what could he want with Fran? He was not shoddy enough to be planning anything disreputable, and she was not high enough for it to have the air of a serious courting. It troubled Mrs. Denver, especially Fran's air of excitement. That was why she had refused to drive out with Mr. Irwin! How contrary the girl was.

"Hyde Park is in the other direction, Lord Devane," Francesca pointed out when Devane headed his horses west on Oxford Street toward Tiburn Road."

"I planned a spin in the country, if that meets with your approval, ma'am," he answered blandly. "Last night I displeased you, carrying on in public. Let my reputation recover before we are seen together."

"Curiously enough, the gentleman's reputation never *does* seem to suffer, does it?" she replied.

"No, it doesn't. There is certainly an inequity in there somewhere."

"An iniquity, I would say."

"You begrudge us our social latitude, do you?" he joked, but listened closely for her reply.

"It has always struck me as very unfair."

"There is an easy way around the injustice for you. Ladies in your position must just be a little more careful. So long as they are married or widowed, they are allowed a fair amount of freedom. It is flaunting their affairs in the face of the world that finishes them."

"I was not talking about myself in particular. I merely think that if gentlemen can misbehave without censure, ladies ought to have the same privilege."

He turned a clever eye on her. "That would be your solution? Some people think gentlemen ought to be forced to behave more properly."

"No one has taught a dog to fly yet, so far as I know." She shrugged.

"You are remarkably lenient, ma'am. You remove the burden of guilt from us. We are doing only as Nature ordained; birds fly, fish swim, and man—alas!—"

Francesca spoke up rapidly to prevent his finishing that questionable speech, "I was not speaking of *all* gentlemen, Lord Devane, but only of rakes— of which I am sure you are not one," she added, blushing, for the conversation was taking a turn she had not anticipated and did not like.

"And men admire beautiful women is what I was going to say," he finished, mockingly demure.

Francesca looked around for a new subject and made do with the weather. "What a lovely day it is." A coven of witch-black birds hovered in the blue sky over a spreading elm, and disappeared into its leafy branches. As they proceeded beyond London, the traffic lessened and greenery stretched on both sides, smiling in the sunlight. Farms and cottages dotted the roadside. Men and horses worked peacefully in the fields. "It reminds me of White Oaks, my home in Surrey," she mentioned. "Where is your home, Lord Devane?"

"In Kent," he answered briefly.

"I think Mr. Irwin mentioned you have another estate as well?"

"Yes, also a hunting box in the Cotswold Hills and a mansion in London. There, it is all on the line," he said, studying her closely. Lord Devane was aware that there were two ways of carrying on affairs. Members of the muslin company expected more in the way of cash. Ladies of quality, unless they were purse-pinched, were allowed the luxury of pretending indifference to money and taking their payment in jewelry. He expected Francesca would fall into the latter category. Her wishing to discuss his assets sounded like fishing to learn what she might get out of him. It displeased him, and when Devane was displeased, his eyebrows pulled into a frown over his eyes.

"You don't seem very pleased about being so wealthy," she charged.

"It does please me. I appreciate money as much as the next one. It allows one the finer things in life."

"This is a very fine carriage," she said. "It hardly jostles at all."

"It is the team that make it seem smoother than it is. And of course the driver," he added with a grin. "Do you drive, Lady Camden?"

"Only the jig, back on Papa's farm. I've never had my own phaeton. My late husband was not so very well off. His father has a good deal of money, I believe, but Lord Maundley is a shocking skint."

He drew off the side of the road, under a tall oak, and turned to her, his expression suddenly serious. Sunlight dappled her face through the moving branches, lending her a restless quality. "It must have been very difficult for you, losing your husband when you were practically newlyweds."

Any mention of David set Francesca's hackles up. She disliked posing as a heartbroken widow, but of course she did not parade his perfidy in front of any but her dearest friends. Even her own family had no idea of it. "It was a trying time," she said in a cool voice.

Devane assumed she was still not totally recovered, and immediately rushed on to speak of other things. "The reason I stopped the carriage, I thought you might like to try the ribbons."

"No, thank you. When I make a fool of myself, I prefer to do it in private."

"I am here to help you."

"Your team is too lively for a beginner."

"I did not expect such reluctance to take a chance from the dashing Frankie Devlin," he jeered.

"I take a chance only when it is myself, or my possessions, that are at stake. The team is yours. If I crippled them, I would be in your debt. I have debts enough without incurring new ones," she added, thinking of the necklace. *I will expect you to make retribution.* David had told her the diamonds were worth five thousand guineas.

So the lady had tumbled into debt! Was that the cause of her straying? "Gambling?" he asked bluntly. His voice was harsh, and his dark eyes stared hard into hers.

"No! I don't gamble beyond a friendly game of whist."

"How did you fall into debt, then?"

His tone, as much as his words, angered her. "Pray, do not concern yourself about my personal problems," she said, holding her head high.

"I hope to make your problems my problems, Lady Camden. I confess, I have an aversion to ladies' gambling beyond their means."

"Another vice reserved for gentlemen," she snipped, eyes flashing. To his considerable astonishment, she completely ignored his hint at shouldering her problems. "Well, are we going to continue this drive, or sit here all day arguing?"

A reluctant smile moved his lips and glowed in the depths of his dark eyes. "A temper! Good. I'm inclined that way myself." He flicked the whip, and the team resumed their smooth trot. Devane instituted some polite conversation on the countryside and social doings.

"There is a quiet inn just along the road here," he said later. "Shall we stop for a drink? Driving in the open air is a thirsty business."

"I would enjoy a drink," she allowed.

The inn, with an ancient brick façade and a thatched roof, looked like a country cottage. Chickens roaming free in the yard added to the impression, and there was no commercial sign at the door to draw in trade. "Are you sure this is an inn?" she asked.

"It is, but it has only three tables. We few who have discovered it keep it a secret. Jed Puckle brews the best ale in England."

A boy came out of the yard and took the reins of the curricle. Devane led Lady Camden through a door so low he had to stoop to enter. It seemed very dark inside, after the bright sunlight. By the light from the windows Francesca saw that the parlor of the house had been converted into a minuscule tap room, holding three deal tables, each with four chairs. Hunting prints decorated the walls, and a dull gleam of pewter vessels enlivened the wooden sideboard. One of the tables was occupied by a pair of gentlemen; the other two were empty.

"Are you sure ladies are allowed here?" she asked, peering all around.

"Quite sure. And even if they weren't, who would see you?"

"A wrong does not consist of getting caught, Lord Devane," she pointed out, but playfully.

"Except in the case of social rules. It cannot be a crime for you to enjoy a drink, even in a men's room. But the room, as I said, is for the use of the general public."

Even as he spoke, a country couple of man and wife came in, laden with parcels, and occupied the last table. "Now you can relax." He reached across the table and patted her hands.

A fresh-faced country wench came and took their order. "Two of your famous ales," Devane said.

"I do not drink ale. May I have tea?" Francesca said.

"But Puckle's ale is famous! I often drive out here for the sole pleasure of tasting it. Two ales and a pot of tea." The girl left.

"My, you are thirsty! Ordering two ales at a time," Francesca said.

"One is for you. I insist you try it."

"I'll try it, but I tell you in advance, I shan't like it."

He leaned across the table and gazed into her eyes. "You should never make up your mind about a thing until you've tried it, Lady Camden." She read some challenge in his words.

The ales and tea were delivered. The dark liquid in the glass Devane held out to her looked lethal. "It tastes better than it looks," he said.

She sipped and found it tasted as bitter and metallic as other ales she had tried. "Sorry, Lord Devane. It is not my cup of tea. This is," she added, reaching for the pot.

He watched, bemused, as she daintily lifted the pot and poured the steaming liquid into the cup. "Well, at least you tried it. It is lacking the fortitude to try new things that is contemptible."

"Like my not laming your team for you?" she asked pertly.

"At least you have driven a jig. A jig is like a cup of tea; driving a team of bloods, on the other hand, is fine wine. I think you are a lady who likes the finer things in life?" His tone made it at least a potential compliment.

Francesca considered it a moment. "I don't know why you say that when I have just settled for tea and a jig. I liked the country very much when I was there. The assemblies, the local beaux, the occasional journeying group of players. Then, when I first went up to London, I became much too grand for country pleasures. But now I am beginning to think I was too hard on country doings. Society is only ordinary people dressed up in silk and jewelry. Their expenses are higher, and their morals lower. Other than that, there isn't really much difference between them so far as I can see."

Devane was silent for a long moment. He had not expected philosophy from a young hellion, much less wisdom. "But would you be happy to go back to the country?"

"Not to my father's house. He is very strict, and he was not happy with my marriage, though he accepted it in the end. Once a lady has been mistress of her own household, she would find it hard to go back to being a dutiful daughter. I am thinking quite seriously of returning to the country nearby and setting up my own household, however, with Mrs. Denver as my companion." Mrs. Denver urged

79

this scheme forward from time to time, and as her troubles increased, it was coming to find some favor with Francesca.

He assumed she was in the suds, and forced to rusticate. "It would be cheaper in the long run, I daresay."

"Oh, it is not a lack of money precisely. Maundley owns the house I live in in London, so that comes free."

Devane blinked in surprise. "I see." A moment's hasty considering told him the young lady might be trying to pressure him into making a proposition immediately. As he watched her sipping her tea, and heard her talking such common sense, it occurred to him that her aim might be marriage rather than a mistress-ship. Marriage had no interest whatsoever for him.

"Do you think you would find amusing friends in the country? You are accustomed now to city flirts."

"I expect that is a reference to our first meeting, at the Pantheon. Major Stanby, the gentlemen I was with, was a new friend. He wanted to marry me. I declined, and he became unpleasantly persistent. I shouldn't have gone there, but I was curious to see all the entertainments of London. Many ladies do go, I believe."

"All the more dashing ones," he agreed. "When the destination is questionable, however, the escort ought to be totally reliable. A wise lady doesn't take on two doubtful factors at the same time."

"Thank you for that tip, Lord Devane." He seemed easy to talk to, and Francesca decided to try a little discreet flirtation. "Now I understand your bringing me to this somewhat questionable spot—because my escort is unexceptionable. That is a compliment, Lord Devane." She smiled.

A flash of white teeth showed in his swarthy face. "Such compliments as that make it very difficult for me to misbehave—on the off chance that I had any such thing in mind."

She laughed lightly. "I doubt you would have come here to do it. It is hardly a bower of bliss. Oh, look, Devane! One of the chickens has gotten into the tap room!"

The hen, a black and white speckled bird, pecked her way across the floor right up to their table, lifted her head, and stared at them with a brightly inquisitive eye.

"I have an aunt who looks like that," Francesca said.

"It reminds me of Countess Lieven."

"Yes, the eyes so sharp. They're good layers, the Speckled Sussex, although they eat more than most chickens." The serving girl rushed in and shooed the bird out the door. "I miss the animals at home," Francesca said in a soft, pensive way. "I had an old dog, Smoky. He was just a mongrel, grayish-blue in color, but very intelligent. We got him to keep the foxes away from the chicken coop, but he developed a taste for eggs himself."

"You had to get rid of him?"

"No, we just kept the henhouse door locked and let him have an occasional cracked egg to eat. Do you like dogs?"

"I have a fine pack of hunting hounds, but I'm not emotionally attached to them. I did have a favorite whelp when I was young, though. She was a terrier. Russet, long ears, sad eyes. She used to hide under the table in the upstairs hall till Papa's bedroom door closed at night, then sneak into my room. She wasn't supposed to be there. She was a good dog, but she used to chew the corners of the feather mattress and scatter the feathers about the room."

"What did you do?"

"Cook put some foul-smelling liquid on the tick, till Yahoo broke her bad habit."

"That's a funny name you called her."

"She *was* a yahoo. No manners, no breeding, but I was fond of her."

They talked about other pets, and childhood experiences. It was not the sort of conversation Devane had in mind when he asked Lady Camden out. After hearing how she had cried for a week when her father drowned some kittens, and admitting to a tear when his donkey was lamed and had to be shot, it seemed hard to even hint at a carte blanche. He decided he would look elsewhere for a mistress, and drove Lady Camden home. She decided he was really very nice when you got to know him. Perhaps it was time to stop paying David back for his sins, and settle down with a new husband.

Lord Devane was worth considering. He had David's unsteady habits, but he was older than David. Perhaps his wild oats were sown, and he would settle down to proper matrimony. At least he was interesting—and of course very eligible.

Chapter Eight

Francesca looked very much like her old carefree
self when she returned from her drive with Lord
Devane. Her cheeks were rosy and her smile was
genuine, not the sardonic smile she so often wore.
Mrs. Denver was sorry to be the bearer of unhappy
tidings, but trouble had arisen during her charge's
absence, and it had been preying on her mind since
Lord Maundley's call an hour before. Before Francesca even removed her bonnet she was called into
the saloon, where a white-faced Mrs. Denver
greeted her.

"What is the matter?" she demanded at once.
"Not Papa! He isn't sick!"

"No, my dear. You had another call from Maundley."

"Oh, that!" she scoffed.

"He as well as accused you of stealing the necklace. He says if it is not returned *immediately*, he
will hand the matter over to the authorities."

Francesca felt a trembling inside. "Let me see
the letter," she said, and reached for the ominous

paper. She unfolded it with trembling fingers and read the curt note.

"I have taken consultation with my solicitor, who advises me I am within my rights to demand immediate return of the Maundley necklace. Failing this, your widow's portion will be docked that sum. In addition, I would like you to vacate my house on Half Moon Street as soon as convenient, but not later than the end of May. I strongly advise you to return the necklace. Your reputation is not sterling enough to bear this additional blow. Sincerely, Lord Maundley."

She handed the note to Mrs. Denver, who quickly perused it.

Lord Maundley had never been friendly, but this note sounded like implacable hatred. And that gratuitous insult about her less than sterling character—that was outrageous. "I have only ten thousand," Francesca said in a hollow voice. "If he takes half, we shan't even be able to afford living here."

"Especially if we have to pay rent besides. We will be quite hard up, even in the country."

"This is infamous!" She stamped her dainty foot in futile vexation.

"You'll have to tell him the truth, Fran."

"I should have told him at the beginning. He wouldn't believe it now. You noticed that jibe about my reputation. Who has been running to him with tales, I wonder."

"What are you going to do?"

Francesca frowned, then her lips firmed, and she said coolly, "I am going to ask Lord Devane's advice."

"Not Devane!"

"Why not? He is the most knowledgeable acquaintance I have. He might discover who David gave the necklace to, and even if he cannot, he will know what I ought to do. He is a man of the world, older, experienced. . . ." She had been wanting to share her problem with him earlier. Had he not shown some willingness to help her when she first indicated obliquely that she was in trouble? She had felt strange, too, accepting his sympathy over David's death, when she now considered it a release rather than a tragedy.

"I think you should speak to Mr. Caine—or perhaps Mr. Irwin might help."

"They have been trying to help all along, Auntie. They mean well, but they lack the drive and power. Selby is out of his depth in any dealings of this sort. Devane will know what to do."

"I don't see what good can come of this, Fran. You hardly know the man. I think we ought to keep the thing as quiet as possible."

"I can trust Devane. He is really very nice, Auntie. We had the loveliest outing, talking about dogs and—oh, he is not at all what I thought. Should I write him a note?" Mrs. Denver pinched her lips and shook her head. "Perhaps that is a little forward. I shall go out this evening and try to find a private moment, or at least ask him to call tomorrow morning. Where are my invitations?" She went to the mantelpiece over the fireplace and picked up a pile of cards, which she shuffled through quickly. "He might be at Lady Jersey's rout, and if not there, I'll try the Grahams' assembly. He's bound to be at one or the other. Did Selby call?"

"Yes, he came in and frowned and swayed for ten minutes, but that was before Maundley's note arrived. He said he would drop around at nine, as usual."

"Excellent. Then he can escort me this evening."

Mrs. Denver was on thorns, but Francesca, strangely, continued relatively unperturbed. She was sure Lord Devane would know just what she should do. No doubt he had encountered thornier problems in the past. And at least, she regretfully admitted, he probably had an intimate acquaintance with the muslin company, and could discover the identity of the mysterious Rita, if he didn't know it already. She would tease him about that, after the matter was settled.

Mrs. Denver had a moment alone with Mr. Caine before she called Francesca down that evening. "So the chickens have come home to roost. She cannot say I didn't warn her," he sighed.

He was as worried as Mrs. Denver, but Francesca seemed almost exultant as she left the house, her hand on his arm. Mr. Caine thought her bird-witted to drag Lord Devane into the imbroglio, but agreed that Devane would have a better chance of both discovering and recovering the necklace than he or Mr. Irwin. "He is not a man whose debt I would care to be in, but at least he never called you a thief" was the most cheerful word she could get out of him.

They ran Lord Devane to ground at their first stop, Lady Jersey's assembly. It was, of course, a squeeze, as any party thrown by a patroness of Almack's was bound to be. Francesca hadn't attended Almack's since David departure. She would not ordinarily have attended such a tonnish do as Lady Jersey's, and assumed that her hostess's cool greeting was a rebuke for abandoning Almack's. Few of her particular friends were there, but she spotted

Devane shortly after she entered the room. His dark head stood above the crowd. He glanced in her direction, but as she was shorter, she thought perhaps he hadn't seen her.

As no other gentleman rushed forward to greet her, she stood up with Mr. Caine for the cotillion. Devane must certainly see her now, and would come to her at the dance's end. When it was over, however, Lord Devane remained with his own set, only changing partners with one of the other gentlemen. Neither did any of her other acquaintances make her welcome. She caught Devane's eye and waved a merry greeting. Devane bowed, and smiled less merrily.

He hoped Lady Camden was not going to become a pest. She had obviously made herself unwelcome at such a polite party as this. One had to wonder why Lady Jersey had invited her. He was at some pains to avoid Francesca till the first intermission. It was at the refreshment parlor that she beckoned to him across the room. He excused himself from his friends and went toward her at a stiff-legged gait.

"Good evening, ma'am," he said, smiling a chilly smile. "Did you wish to speak to me?"

His cool manner made Francesca uncomfortable, but she forged ahead. "I would like a private word with you, if that is possible."

His smile dwindled to a questioning frown. "This is hardly the optimum time or place for private conversation."

"Perhaps you could call on me tomorrow, then."

"I fear tomorrow I shall be in Newmarket, Lady Camden. I suggest you take up your problem with Mr. Caine, or perhaps Lord Maundley. Good evening." He bowed civilly enough. "Nice meeting you again." Then he was gone.

Francesca stood with Selby, her cheeks stained scarlet. She caught her lower lip between her teeth to hold back the tears of shame. She had been boasting to Mrs. Denver and Selby how nice Devane was, and this was the way he treated her. He would not treat a stranger so shabbily. Why had he done it?

She gave a flounce of her shoulders and said, "Let us go." She took Mr. Caine by the arm and strode angrily from the room, without nodding to a single guest, or even thanking her hostess.

As the final embarrassment, she met Lord Devane at the door, awaiting his carriage. He was fleeing from her, too. "It is a busy evening," he said, somewhat ashamed. "The height of the Season—there are half a dozen parties to visit tonight."

"Don't let us detain you," Lady Camden said through stiff lips, and without looking at him.

"My carriage has not arrived yet." He saw her agitation and felt a moment's pang at his rough usage. Perhaps it was some quite simple thing she wanted—a voucher to Almack's, or an introduction to someone. "What was it you wanted to speak to me about, Lady Camden?" he asked warily.

She gave him one quick, angry glare. "Nothing I cannot ask of a *friend* instead. Sorry to trouble you." She turned her shoulder on him and spoke to Selby until Devane's carriage arrived. He looked at her then, planning to say good evening, but she refused to see him.

He felt a disquieting sense of having behaved badly as the carriage took him to Mrs. Graham's ball. Lady Camden would very likely be there. He would find a moment to apologize, and discover what she wanted. She was not the sort of lady he wished to have much to do with; too respectable for dalliance and too raffish for anything more serious, but that was not to say he should be rude to her.

He soon learned she was not at Lady Graham's. He did hear her name mentioned, however. An ugly rumor was overheard involving her in some brouhaha about a diamond necklace. Old Maundley was in the boughs about it. Lady Camden, it seemed, had refused to return it to him when her husband died. As she had no heir to inherit the thing, he supposed it ought, by rights, to go back to Maundley until the younger son reached his maturity, though he thought the man a boor to insist on it. Why not let her wear it for the nonce? The new heir was only a schoolboy and would have no need of it for a decade.

Devane left the party early, and continued on to a different rout. The necklace story was making the rounds there, too. A Mrs. McGillis nabbed Devane at the corner of the dance floor and whispered in his ear. "If Lady Camden has the thing, why not give it back? I'll tell you what *I* think. She's sold it. Probably to pay her gambling debts."

"I don't believe the lady gambles, except for a friendly game of whist." His tone invited the lady to either explain or retract her statement.

"She does everything else she shouldn't," Mrs. McGillis replied knowingly. "A shocking flirt, milord. She uses men up like linen. Uses them awhile, then flings them aside. Old Maundley is fed up with her. He is going to put her out of her house, did you hear? He obviously knows something the rest of us don't, or why would he treat her so harshly?"

"I cannot believe he would be so vindictive."

"No more he would if there weren't a good reason," she said sapiently.

The lady left, to pour her tale into other ears. Devane withdrew to a quiet corner to digest what he had heard. If Lady Camden was indeed the grasping sort of woman this story suggested, he was glad he hadn't become involved with her. She had indicated that afternoon that she was in some financial trouble, but when he had urged her to confide, she had shut up like a clam. That didn't look as if she was trying to use him.

Yet this evening she had sought his help. Surely this necklace business was what she wished to discuss with him. He went over their conversation, looking for clues as to her thinking. She had mentioned retiring to the country. Was that a hint that she required a patron? Under the present circumstances, she could hardly have expected any other sort of offer.

Would the fun-loving Frankie Devlin really want to retire from society? More likely, she had sold the entailed necklace to pay her debts, gambling or otherwise, and wanted him to buy it back in return for her favors. A bauble like the Maundley diamonds would be worth several thousand guineas. A bit steep . . . But then, Lady Camden was something rather out of the ordinary. Considering the problem without the facts was pointless. He would call on Lady Camden tomorrow and learn the truth from her. When his decision was taken, he put the matter at the back of his mind and continued on to another party, where he enjoyed a flirtation with a different lady.

Mr. Caine took Lady Camden straight home. She

went to her room immediately, and Mrs. Denver spoke to Mr. Caine. "What happened to her? She looks like death."

"She had her say to Devane. You see the result. The man has no more interest in her than in a flea. I don't know where she got the notion he is nice. He couldn't have been ruder. He all but cut her dead."

"How very odd."

Weaving was not enough release of Selby's nerves on this occasion. He paced the room instead. "I begin to wonder if word of Maundley's stunt isn't circulating in society already. Fran was too absorbed in Devane to notice, but I saw several ladies at the assembly looking at her askance and whispering behind their fans. Lady Jersey herself, that renowned chatterbox, was noticeably silent. Nothing would cool Devane's interest more quickly than a sordid scandal. Very likely that is behind his suddenly becoming an icicle."

"The poor girl. She won't dare show her nose outside of the house. Whatever can we do, Mr. Caine?"

"If we don't do something, her reputation will be in shreds. I think I ought to go and have a word with Lord Maundley." He stopped pacing and turned back to her. "What do you think?"

"You would tell him about David and that Rita woman?" she asked uncertainly.

"I don't see any other way out of this imbroglio. Did you keep the letters?"

"No, Fran threw them into the fire."

"A pity. It leaves us with no proof. Still, it's worth a try."

"Fran was most eager to spare Lady Maundley grief. Could you ask him not to tell his wife?"

"He shouldn't need telling, but I'll explain that that is the reason Fran hasn't spoken before now. This is not an interview I am looking forward to," he said, frowning deeply to consider it.

"Most unpleasant. Will you return this evening and tell me what Maundley had to say?"

"Indeed I shall. It shouldn't take long."

Mr. Caine left, and Mrs. Denver remained belowstairs, waiting for him. She was so agitated she had a large glass of sherry, which helped very little. She knew Fran would be unhappy with the action being taken behind her back, but really there was no other way out of this quagmire. Once she heard that Maundley had backed down and apologized, she would be so relieved she would thank Mr. Caine.

No forty-five minutes ever seemed so long or so ghastly as the forty-five minutes Mrs. Denver waited for Mr. Caine's return. Fear clutched at her heart, making it ache in her chest. She couldn't take much more of this sort of carrying-on. If Fran was to continue on in London, she would have to find another companion. Much as she loved the girl, she could not ride herself into the grave.

At last the tap at the door came, and Mrs. Denver herself answered it. She knew by Mr. Caine's frown that he had met with no success. "Was he not at home?" she asked eagerly.

They went into the saloon, and Mr. Caine resumed his pacing back and forth. "He was home right enough, but he didn't believe a word I said. Where were the letters from these alleged mistresses of his son's, he wanted to know. Why had Lady Camden not told him sooner? Before I left, the word *slander* was being flung at my head. He used phrases like 'dishonoring the memory of a hero, who is not alive to defend himself.' 'If Lady Camden breathes a word of this salacious lie, I will take her to court for the lying thief she is.' Those were his last words. I wouldn't stay to hear more. I am not a violent man, Mrs. Denver, but it was all I could do to keep my fists off him."

Mrs. Denver's face was ashen. "What can the poor girl do?"

"Nothing. Maundley is the guardian of her trust fund. He will dock it for five thousand and put her out of this house. How will that leave Fran fixed financially?"

"Just five thousand left. She hasn't another *sou* in the world, and she would never approach her papa for more. But can Maundley take her money? That was her dowry. It didn't come from Camden. He gave her nothing but his title, and a life of misery."

"When she married, the money became Camden's by law. Fortunately Sir Gregory got a promise out of Camden that if anything happened to him, the money would revert to Fran, no strings attached."

"This is so unfair!"

"Indeed it is. Justice is an illusion. And the whole town will believe Maundley's lies if they don't already. It quite kills Fran's chance of ever making a respectable alliance. I think the only thing to do is take her home to her father."

"She'd never go, Mr. Caine. Nor could I ask her to. She was not happy there, and with this new twist her papa would rag the poor child to death. No, we must manage to live somehow on the interest of five thousand pounds."

"That will hardly pay her rent, to say nothing of servants and daily living expenses."

"She must cut her coat to fit the cloth. She could eke out a respectable existence in the country, I expect."

"Yes, in hired rooms, or a little cottage," he replied glumly. He took a deep breath and said, "Do you think I ought to offer for her?"

The question obviously cost him something. Mrs. Denver shook her head. "You have already done more than enough, Mr. Caine. Marriages of that sort never work out. I'll let her sleep tonight and give her the bad news in the morning."

"I'll come around to see if there is anything I can do to help."

"You have been very kind. I don't know what we would have done without you."

Her desolate expression was a tacit admission that even with him, affairs had reached an impossible state. Mrs. Denver went up to bed and spent a sleepless night trying to make plans for the future. Some secret corner of her heart was half relieved that Fran would have to leave London. The girl would be bitter, of course, but at least she would be away from the sort of fast company encountered here. The sort of company that could bring a simple country girl to utter ruin. Company like Lord Maundley, and Lord Devane.

Chapter Nine

Lord Maundley was in a fury, and in his wrath he did not hesitate to blacken Lady Camden's character as she traduced the memory of his son. He did not believe a word the lying thief said against David. She had been nothing but grief to his family. A nobody out of the country, when David might have had a duke's daughter, and she hadn't even given him a son. He went straight to his solicitor in the morning and instituted the legal proceedings to seek payment for the necklace. He would not see the woman again. It was all up to the law now, and the sooner the world knew what she was, the better.

Lady Camden went down to breakfast late that morning. Her face was pale, and purple smudges below her eyes spoke of a sleepless night. She seemed strangely apathetic, even when Mrs. Denver admitted that Mr. Caine had called on Lord Maundley.

"I'm sure you both meant it for the best, Auntie," she said in a flat voice. Her eyes snapped when she heard the names Maundley had called her, but even that she took without resorting to hysterics. "One always considers the source of an insult," she said with one of her shrugs.

Mrs. Denver did not point out that the source, in this case, was the highly prestigious Lord Maundley. Mr. Caine came to call, as promised.

After a few moments' general repining, he got down to business. "I have been thinking about this wretched affair, and what you must do is hire yourself a lawyer, Fran, and a good one. You'll be bitten to death by the fees, but you must defend yourself. You'll need character witnesses; I shall be happy to speak on your behalf. And we shall have to find people to confirm that David was not Simon Pure."

Lady Camden's lips curled in distaste. Drag all the dirty family linen through court? "If Lord Maundley is that eager to steal my five thousand pounds, let him. I shan't appear in court. It is too degrading."

Mr. Caine urged her to stand up for herself, but Mrs. Denver was hesitant. "Maundley would drag in that Fran has been running around with a dozen young men," she mentioned. "There is no denying that, Mr. Caine. All perfectly innocent, of course, but it won't look that way. Much better to just let him take the money, and we shall retire into the country."

"There is something in what you say. A reputation cannot be bought at any price."

"No," Francesca said calmly. "What we must do is find the necklace."

"We've already tried that," Mr. Caine reminded her.

"It wasn't pawned at Stop Hole Abbey, so the

woman must still have it. I must discover the identity of Rita, and recover the necklace. I shall take it to Lord Maundley and throw it in his face—in public. Perhaps in front of the House of Lords," she said, smiling a malicious smile.

"Yes, and he'll say you had it all along," Mr. Caine pointed out. "How do you plan to find the necklace?"

"I have no idea. I must think about it, and come up with a plan." On this brave speech she thanked Mr. Caine most kindly, and left.

"Any plan to find the cursed thing will involve her with the muslin company. In her present mood, I dread to think what she has in mind," Mr. Caine said, worried.

"The sooner we get her out of London, the better," Mrs. Denver said. "We'll get her far enough away that she can't be running back to make more mischief. Somewhere in Surrey, perhaps, but not too close to her home. Close enough to visit her family, I mean, but not to be overwhelmed by them. I expect we should go and visit an estate agent who deals in country properties."

"Weber's, on Coventry Street," Mr. Caine said. "Meanwhile, I wonder if she would like to visit my sister. Mary would like to have her, I'm sure. They haven't seen each other since Fran and I stood godparents to Harry. It would get Fran's mind off all this bother."

"That's a good idea. I'll suggest it. Shall I go to Weber's, Mr. Caine, or ..."

"Why don't we both go now, while she is busy? She won't come up with a plan before lunch, I shouldn't think."

"I'll just get my pelisse. I'll tell the servants we

97

are going to the lending library, in case Fran comes down and asks."

Lord Devane went on the strut on Bond Street that morning to replenish his supply of snuff and talk to his friends. He was particular about his snuff. He favored the light character of Martinique, which he strengthened with one tenth part of the powerful, large-grained Brazil. As he strolled through the shop, he read the labels on the glazed jars: Macouba, Spanish Bran, Violet Strasbourg—a lady's snuff. Beside and around him, the low rumble of gossips at work could be overheard. The only *on-dit* on anyone's lips was the Lady Camden affair. Frankie had really pitched herself into the suds this time.

"Poor girl, I can almost pity her. Whatever will she do?"

"She'll have to leave town, won't she? Mean to say, old Maundley's kicking her out of the house. If I were her, I'd be gone by now. No one wants to be the butt of cartoons and public jokes."

A quiver of apprehension shot through Devane. He had been making his plans and had decided to let Lady Camden stew a few days in this broth of her own concocting, but it was possible she might leave town before he spoke to her. He bought his snuff and went out to leap into his curricle, which his tiger had awaiting him. "Half Moon Street," he called, and let his man take the reins, to allow him to prepare his speech. A little apology for last night's brusqueness for openers. Some excuse for being still in town, when he had claimed a trip to Newmarket. A fleeting, oblique mention of the trouble she found herself in. He would not dwell on it or rub it in. He hoped she didn't cry. He despised watering pots. But of course she would be deeply troubled, and that is when he would broach his plan of rescue.

He meant to be not only generous, but lavish. He would pay for the stolen necklace, and set her up in style in London. Her reputation would not suffer in the least, rather, the contrary. She was a widow, not a deb. Officially, they would be good friends, but within the inner circle, people would know the relationship between them. This need not prevent Lady Camden from being accepted everywhere. Adultery was tolerated when it was executed with style and discretion. When their affair was over, she would be free to marry where she wished. Much better off than she was now. Yes, she would certainly jump at his offer.

No fear of rejection bothered Lord Devane when he lifted the brass knocker of the tall, narrow house on Half Moon Street. Not much of a house; he would do better for her. "Lord Devane to see Lady Camden," he said when the butler answered.

The butler had not been aware of Lord Devane's odium, and went to the saloon to announce him to Lady Camden, who had just come down. Probably expecting his lordship, the butler surmised. From the hallway Devane heard himself being announced. A dead silence followed. After a long moment Lady Camden's voice was heard. "I am not at home to Lord Devane, Palter."

Francesca was in a fury and made no effort to lower her voice. Let him hear her deny him entry. How *dare* he come here, after the way he had treated her!

"Very good, madam."

Palter turned to leave and found himself confronted with the very tall, wide-shouldered noble-man wearing a sardonic grin. "Thank you, Palter," Devane said, and strolled into the saloon. Palter gave one helpless look and left, shaking his head.

Devane bowed punctiliously and spoke in polite accents. "I am sorry to hear you are indisposed, Lady Camden."

She rose up from the sofa, pale as a wraith, her features frozen in disbelief. In her white face her eyes were like banked coals. "Get out!" she said.

Devane continued toward her. "I have come to apologize for last night's brusque injury. You may imagine how I felt, to see you with Mr. Caine— again." It came to him as an inspiration, to pretend jealousy.

"Out, I say!" she exclaimed, pointing a finger to the door.

"Let me speak my piece. Every dog has his bite, and we are confirmed dog-lovers, you and I. Come now, there is no need for such Draconian treatment as this, Francesca."

Slightly mollified by his apology, and extremely curious, she sat down. Devane sat on the chair nearest her and reached for her hand. This was do-ing it a bit brown, and Francesca withdrew her fin-gers. "Say what you have to say, and go," she said coolly.

"I came about the necklace," he said, and watched her closely. Yes, that got to her.

She looked at him, a helpless yet hopeful glance. "Oh, you have heard about it."

It was all the encouragement he needed. He rose and joined her on the sofa, an avuncular arm around her shoulders. "Poor girl. All of London knows. Nothing else is spoken of on Bond Street

100

this morning." She drew in a sharp breath and moved a little away. The skin on her pale face seemed to tighten visibly. She bit her lips, and looked a question at him. "That was what you wished to discuss last night, I collect?" he asked gently.

"Yes. I was going to ask your help." She looked at him uncertainly.

"Naturally I am eager to help, but I could not dislike to discuss it so publicly."

"But you said you would be at Newmarket today."

"I didn't go when I saw you needed me."

A hesitant smile hovered on her lips, and her eyes softened. "Oh, is that what it was: I found it hard to believe you could have changed so completely, so quickly."

"My feelings have not changed, Francesca. Do you mind if I call you so?" She just smiled, and he continued. "You recall I said I was eager to help, and indeed I am."

"Oh, thank you. Maundley is being perfectly *dreadful*! He is stealing my money, and making me leave the house."

"Then he must be dealt with. I won't have you badgered in this fashion. You must leave Maundley up to me."

It felt like the weight of the world falling from her shoulders. Tears glazed her eyes, and she could think of no words to say. She had always felt, almost by instinct, that Devane could handle anything. "Thank you," she said softly.

Through the blur of tears she saw his head bending toward hers, but there was no menace in his aspect. His face was softened with pleasure as he smiled at her. His lips alighted on hers, as gentle as the brush of a butterfly's wing. His arms closed around her, still gently, but the kiss deepened.

Francesca felt she was in a dream. Devane was going to rescue her. He loved her. His arms tightened, and she put her arms around him, returning the pressure. The embrace quickly escalated from tenderness to rising passion. Suddenly Devane was crushing the air out of her lungs, and Francesca was shocked to notice that she was reciprocating. She drew back, breathing hard, and embarrassed.

"What will you think of me?" she asked with a trembling smile.

"I think you are the most delightful lady I have ever had the pleasure of meeting—and assisting in her troubles. Maundley is putting you out of the house, you said. We shall just have to remove you to a different house. I must say, I don't think much of his provison for his daughter-in-law."

"He was always clutch-fisted," she sniffed.

"Older men are not so easily influenced by a young lady's charms," he said blandly. "Now, about this wretched necklace. Where is it?"

"I don't know. I believe my husband gave it to his mistress."

A sharp look pierced her. "Come now, if you want my help, you must play fair with me, Francesca. I will repay Maundley for the trinket, or I will return it and buy you a new one, but between us there will be no prevarication."

She began to sense some undertone of duplicity in his kind offer. "I couldn't let you pay for it. It costs five thousand guineas. I was hoping you would help me discover who David gave it to, and get it back."

"I think we both know who he gave it to," he said with a cynical look.

"Indeed I do not. Why would I ask your help if I knew?"

"Because I am rich, and I like you. I think you and I would deal very well together, but I insist on the truth."

Francesca's heart soared an instant, but the word *like*, when added to his cool expression, did not hint at a proposal. "What, exactly, did you have in mind, Lord Devane?"

"A house in the West End, a generous allowance, every consideration for your reputation, and a settlement one way or the other regarding the necklace. I doubt you will find many gentlemen as generous."

Her ears rang, and her head felt light. "A mistress-ship, in fact."

He inclined his head slightly in agreement.

He hadn't even the grace to blush, but examined her as if she were a heifer up for auction. "You will please leave this house at once. I will not tell Mr. Caine what you have suggested, or he would insist on calling you out, and I would not like anyone killed because of me. If word of this infamous insult is bruited about town, however, he will undoubtedly challenge you to a duel. And he is a very fair shot, too," she added, although she doubted Selby had ever held a pistol in his life.

Devane heard her out without any particular show of outrage. "Surely you didn't expect an offer of marriage?"

She blushed, but denied it. "I did not. I thought you were offering the assistance of a disinterested friend. Neither did I expect this—this—outrage!"

103

Devane got to his feet. "You are warm in your treatment of disinterested friends. After you have considered this outrage in quiet contemplation, you may change your tune. You are a byword for profligacy in this town, Frankie."

Her cheeks turned to scarlet, but she held back the tears. They glittered like mica in her eyes, but did not fall. "That is what appealed to you, no doubt."

He gave a shrug of his shoulders. "As you see. You are on the point of being ejected from your house, your money greatly reduced, your reputation in ruins. You told me earlier you have no wish to return to your father's house. What other option is open to you?"

"And you, in your kindness, have come to take advantage of a helpless lady. My God, I thought David was bad. At least he did not prey on decent women. I would sooner milk cows or wash dishes for a living than live with you."

"Why, I think we would deal admirably. A widow who maligns the character of her dead husband, who plays the coquette with such easy abandon and sets the seal on her sterling character by stealing the family jewels can hardly expect a carte blanche from a vicar. You will not receive another offer so generous."

"I do not consider any offer outside of marriage generous, sir. And if you can believe all that of me, I wonder that you make any offer at all."

"I am not interested in your character. In fact, I rather like an accomplished flirt."

"Flirts are more demanding. We demand at least a token of common decency. Good day."

She didn't bother asking him to leave again. She

left herself instead, with a withering glare as she swept past him, holding her skirts aside to avoid contamination.

Devane sat on a minute, thinking. He had certainly botched that in some manner! It had seemed to begin auspiciously enough. Surely she didn't think he had come to offer marriage to someone who had made herself the talk of the town? But that, obviously, was exactly what she did think despite her mention of disinterested friendship. That kiss had no reek of friendship, yet she had been truly disgusted at his proposition. A very foolish brain resided inside that girl's head. He rose slowly and left, for although he had not an iota of fear for Mr. Caine's shooting ability, he had no wish to involved himself in a rackety duel.

Devane went to his club to catch up on the latest gossip regarding the Lady Camden affair. He met Mr. Irwin and accosted him as a likely source of information. "I owe you a drink, Mr. Irwin," he said.

Mr. Irwin smiled in agreement. "We shall continue our discussion that was interrupted by my darting off t'other night."

They went to a table and called for wine. "Something to do with a diamond necklace, and Stop Hole Abbey, I think you said? That sounds amusing. Tell me about it."

"I daresay there is no harm in telling it, now that the whole town is buzzing with Maundley's version of the story. The thing is, you see, that loose screw of a Camden gave the family diamonds to his mistress, and old Maundley has got the wind up that Lady Camden took them."

"Surely that is what the whole town thinks."

"Aye, because Maundley said so, and Lady Camden was too green to hold on to the evidence to the contrary. She found billets-doux in Camden's effects when she was clearing the debris away after his death. Silly ass was carrying on with a girl called Rita and squirreled away her notes. Stands to reason he gave the wench the diamonds. I daresay he thought he'd be home and recover them before they were missed, but then he caught a bullet in the Peninsula—and he only a civil servant—and that is what put the cat among the pigeons."

"Did Lady Camden not tell Lord Maundley about this?"

"She didn't want his parents to know what a scoundrel he was. Maundley was told by Caine when he began threatening her, but he didn't believe it then. Maybe if Lady Camden had gone to him with the notes in the first place—but she didn't realize then that the diamonds were missing, you see, and there was no point upsetting his parents. Maundley won't hear a word against Camden now."

Devane listened closely and said, "It is no secret that Camden carried on his affairs, even after his marriage. I seem to recall a Mrs. Ritchie."

"No, it wasn't her. It was some woman called Rita he was seeing. That's how she signed her billets-doux. I've been trying to get a line on her, but you know the sort of freemasonry that exists within the muslin company."

"Still, if this story is true," Devane said pensively, "it shouldn't be impossible to discover the woman's identity. Very likely she still has the bauble. She could hardly sell a famous necklace, not to a reputable jeweler, at any rate."

"No, and not to Stop Hole Abbey either. I've been

there. Well, that's where I was off to the evening we met."

"To try to recover Lady Camden's diamonds."

"No, Lord Maundley's," he replied with a worried frown. "A simple greenhead like Lady Camden, she isn't capable of dealing with a cut-and-thrust gent like Maundley."

"I would hardly call her a greenhead."

"Well, she is," Mr. Irwin said firmly. "She never had a beau till Camden. He brought her to London fresh from the depths of Surrey. She was mad for him. Of course she was cut to ribbons when he got killed, but until she found out he had other women, she was still as faithful as if he were alive. It was only when she learned the truth that she began to cut up her larks in revenge. Innocent larks, Devane. As innocent as the flirting of a deb. Still, as she ain't a deb, but a widow, some tongues began wagging. The worst of it is, there are wretches in this town who would take advantage of a lady in her position."

Devane sipped his wine in silence, but he felt decidedly uneasy to hear himself called a wretch.

"And who has she got to defend her?" Mr. Irwin continued. "Mr. Caine—another greenhead, when all's said and done. He wouldn't know what to do with a bit o' muslin if she dropped her hankie in his path. He'd pick it up and give it back and continue on his way."

"Who, exactly, is this Mr. Caine, and what is his relationship to her?"

"He's a friend and neighbor from Surrey. A sort of surrogate brother. Lady Camden and his young sister were bosom bows. Caine is about fed up with the whole thing. I was speaking to him this morning. He hopes to get her packed off to the country."

"He is not a suitor, then?"

"No, he'll marry some bishop's daughter, if he ever finds one desperate enough to have him."

"Hmm. If Lady Camden leaves town with this cloud hanging over her head, she will never be able to return."

"She'll be leaving, right enough. Old Maundley is kicking her out of his house and docking her dowry the price of the necklace. It'll leave her too short to carry on in London even if she wanted to."

"Are you an old friend of Lady Camden's?" Devane asked, to insure that the man knew what he was talking about.

"No, I just met her, but I've known Selby Caine for donkey's years. We were at Harrow and Oxford together. Salt of the earth. He wouldn't have the imagination to lie, even if he had the inclination, which he don't. Besides, you've only to spend five minutes with Fran—Lady Camden—to know she's still wet behind the ears."

Devane had a sharp mental image of a chicken walking up to his table at Puckle's and Francesca smiling at it. She had mentioned the breed and gone on to talk about her home. He had been sure, that day, that she was what she said she was. "So what is to be done?" he murmured more to himself than to his companion.

"Maundley's already doing it, isn't he? He's hired a solicitor and charged her with theft."

"My meaning is, what is to be done to recover the necklace?"

"You have me there. I've done what I can, but I meet a stone wall, Devane. The necklace is hidden

108

away in a vault somewhere, or chopped up and the stones sold separately."

Devane took his decision and rose suddenly. "Thanks for the drink."

"You bought it."

"Ah, then, thank you for your delightful company, and the information."

"Where are you off to, Devane?"

"I have to see a woman about a diamond."

Guilt and shame warred in Devane's heart as he went to call his curricle. He had dishonored a respectable lady, a lady in devastating trouble. And he, with all the grace of a wounded elephant, had gone stampeding in, trying to take advantage of her. Honor demanded that he repay this outrage against womanhood. He could only wonder that Caine and Irwin between them couldn't accomplish such a trifling objective, yet he was happy they had not. The return of the diamond necklace would be his apology to Lady Camden. Perhaps, one day, she would even forgive him.

Chapter Ten

"Nonsense!" Lady Camden declared when Mrs. Denver and Mr. Caine returned with news of a cottage for hire in Crawley, close, but not too close, to her ancestral home. "If I run away, everyone will think I am guilty. I must stay and clear my name."

"How do you propose to do that?" Mrs. Denver demanded.

"I have friends. I shall put all my friends on the alert to learn what they can of David's bit o' muslin. Someone is bound to know who she is. I have been too backward, until now, trying to spare Lady Maundley. The Maundleys are sparing me nothing, so I shall mount a concerted attack."

"Even if you discover who she is, Fran, the woman will have the thing hidden away in a vault. You'll never prove David gave it to her," Mr. Caine pointed out.

"I'll worry about that when I learn who she is," she replied mutinously. "I will *not* have horrid people saying I am a thief, and worse. The first friend who calls to offer comfort, I shall enlist his—or her—aid."

The door knocker remained adamantly silent throughout the morning. Mrs. Denver and Mr. Caine extolled in vain the virtues of a Queen Anne cottage at Crawley, and some peace and quiet.

"We seem to have plenty of both here," Francesca scowled. Some part of her did want to escape the awful worries that engulfed her, but she would not allow the likes of Lord Devane to blacken her name without at least trying to clear herself. As soon as she had cleared her name, however, she would retire permanently from London.

"What about a visit to Mary?" Mr. Caine suggested, hoping the word *visit* might be less despised than *moving away*.

"I should enjoy it very much—after I find the necklace."

Mr. Caine remained to lunch because he did not like to see poor Mrs. Denver left alone with her unmanageable charge. The woman looked on the verge of a breakdown. At two-thirty the long-awaited sound of the knocker was heard, and Francesca gave a smile of triumph. "I told you my friends would not desert me." She would not let herself think, for even an instant, that it was Lord Devane come to apologize.

It was Mr. Irwin who was shown in, and her sinking heart told her that hope had risen, despite her better judgment. "I came to see if I could offer any consolation at this trying time," he said, as if entering a house of death.

Mr. Caine, willingly assuming the role of chief mourner, replied, "Very kind of you, John. Pray, have a seat."

"You can offer more than condolences, sir. You can offer to help me," Lady Camden said, and indicated a seat by her side.

"Nothing would give me greater pleasure, ma'am. Only say the word."

"A drive, that is the word," she replied. "Take me for a drive in the park. I want to meet my friends, and try if I can gain a circle of supporters."

"Upon my word, she's mad," Mr. Caine said aside to Mrs. Denver.

Mr. Irwin looked aghast. "You want to go into public! I cannot think that is a good idea, Lady Camden. There are rumors swirling on every side. It would be very uncomfortable for you—people staring and whispering."

"I have not done anything wrong. I won't be driven into a hole by vicious gossip-mongers. Will you take me, or must I go alone?" Her bold, haughty look indicated that she would tackle even that.

Mr. Irwin looked to the others, who were too weary to continue the argument. "Go ahead," Mrs. Denver said. "Let her see for herself what she is facing."

"But I am driving my open carriage."

"Good," Francesca said.

When she went to her room to tidy her hair, she hardly recognized the pale, ravaged face in the mirror. The rouge pot restored her color, and her most dashing chipped-straw bonnet shadowed her eyes, to partially conceal their haunted stare. But her lips drooped wearily. She couldn't take much more of this. Perhaps she should retire. It was only Devane's sneering, hateful face that gave her the strength to carry on. She would have an apology from that creature if she had to personally tour every stew and brothel in London to find the necklace.

With her chin high she went belowstairs, wearing a brightly feverish smile. "All set!"

She realized from the first block that the drive was going to be an ordeal. Her very neighbors averted their heads to avoid nodding, and in this less than choice neighborhood she was one of very few noble ladies. Her neighbors used to lower their windows and crane their necks, hoping she would stop for a word.

"Commoners!" Mr. Irwin said in derision.

"Let us drive along Piccadilly and down to St. James's Park. We will meet half of London there."

Before they had gone far they met a carriage holding Sir Edmund and Lady Greer, old friends from Francesca's first Season in town. They pointedly averted their eyes and looked the other way.

"They are more David's friends than mine," Lady Camden explained. "Maundley has gotten to them."

The next carriage held newer friends, met since David's death. Mrs. Siskins nodded her head a quarter of an inch, but with such a frosty expression that she might as well not have bothered. Her husband looked right through them. The story was repeated, with slight variations, at every carriage they met.

When they reached the Mall, Mr. Irwin said, "Have you had enough? Shall we go home?"

It was a strong temptation, but desperation lent Francesca courage. "No, I might as well go all the way. If this is how it is going to be, I must know. Do you mind?"

"In for a penny," Mr. Irwin said resignedly, and

jiggled the reins. He felt sorry for Lady Camden, but he was also worried about his own reputation. Still, there was some gallantry in standing by a lady in distress. The worst that could be said was that he was a gullible fool taken in by an Incomparable. There was some romance in that.

Things seemed to be improving once they entered the park. Traffic was heavy, and they did not feel they were standing out so noticeably. None of the carriages stopped, but Miss Perkins had her driver slow down, and said through the window, "I am so sorry, Frankie. Truly I am." Her words trailed behind her as the carriage trotted by.

Mr. Irwin heard a sniffle, and felt his heart would break. "This is enough. I'm taking you home, I won't have you patronized by snips like Miss Perkins and insulted by everyone else."

"Yes, please," she said in a dying voice.

"Damme, there is Devane!"

Francesca's head jerked up, and she espied in the distance, advancing toward them, Devane's gleaming yellow curricle and dashing team of grays. She schooled her features to composure, and took a glance at his companion. What she saw caused her blood to freeze. It was a redhead of outstanding beauty. Not Maria Mondale, but Mrs. Ritchie, David's old flirt. One would think Devane had done it on purpose. He had caught her eye, and was staring. He could not fail to see the carriage in front of him, whose passengers cut her dead. She felt her shame was complete.

Devane did not stop his carriage or even slow his pace, but as he passed, he nodded and said in a loud, friendly voice, "Good afternoon, Lady Camden. Lovely day."

She gave him the cut direct. It was the ultimate humiliation that he should see her in her disgrace. "Turn at the next corner and take me home, please."

"Why, things are picking up! That was Devane, and he spoke in quite a civil way. If he hadn't been with that woman, I daresay he would have stopped a moment."

"Is that his new flirt?"

"Must be. He doesn't have a mistress at the moment. He is seen about with various females. That one is not a lightskirt precisely, though she behaves like one. I have seen her about here and there at quite respectable parties."

"I know who she is. I just didn't know if she is Devane's mistress. Her name is Mrs. Ritchie."

"He always chooses the prettiest ladies—er, women."

The only possible reply was to laugh, but as the laughter rose higher, and assumed a tinge of hysteria, Mr. Irwin feared his companion was about to go into a swoon. He pulled under the shelter of a spreading elm till she had settled down, then drove her home. She sat, listless, in the carriage, not even looking to see whether passersby nodded or spoke. She might as well have been asleep for all she noticed or cared.

Her mind was busy with other things. It hadn't taken Devane long to find a new mistress. Francesca had found it strange that he cared for herself in that way, but now she saw that he shared David's unaccountably catholic tastes in women. Bad as David was, he knew the difference between a lady and a woman like Mrs. Ritchie, who could be bought, if the price was right. David had offered marriage at least.

When she was delivered back to Half Moon Street, she went directly to her room, like one in a trance. Mr. Irwin remained behind to explain to Mrs. Denver and Selby. "How did it go?" Mrs. Denver asked fearfully.

"As bad as it possibly could. An unmitigated disaster."

"I've seen it coming. Fran brought it on herself, when all's said and done," Mr. Caine added, and swayed with a slow, measured rhythm, while staring into the grate.

"There may be one advantage to it," Mr. Irwin pointed out. "I doubt she will want to remain in town now."

"I'll go up to her," Mrs. Denver said.

"Let her be. I think she wants to be alone. Perhaps you could send up some brandy."

"Oh, dear! As bad as that?"

"She was holding together till we met Devane and Mrs. Ritchie, and then—"

"Mrs. Ritchie!" Caine exclaimed. "Good God, that is what did the mischief. She was David's woman."

"Not the one who snaffled the diamonds?" Mr. Irwin asked.

"No, the one before that."

"Ah."

Mr. Irwin left, feeling he had done all that friendship demanded, and a good deal more. He thought he might meet Devane at his club, and encourage him in his support of Lady Camden. Devane was not there, however.

He was much more usefully employed in quizzing Mrs. Ritchie to learn who her successor in Lord

Camden's favor had been. Mrs. Ritchie was vague, except in establishing who had given whom his congé. "After I dropped Camden, he ran around with half a dozen girls, but he finally took up with a blond female."

"He liked variety."

"Anything but brunettes, in his friends. His wife is a brunette, you must know. Perhaps he wanted to forget her," she laughed.

Devane swallowed his ire and said, "You don't remember the girl's name, or anything about her?"

She gave him a flirtatious glance from the corner of her infamous green eyes. "Why, milord, one would think you are already wearied of redheads."

"Never. But about the blonde . . ."

"I associate very little with such common garden-variety females as the one you are interested in. She was from the Lake District, I think someone mentioned."

Devane saw that Mrs. Ritchie resented being put into the same category as acknowledged mistresses. She still clung to a shred of respectability. Nor would she tell him anything, so long as she feared competition from the blonde. No doubt it had galled her when Camden dropped her for the other woman, and she would enjoy her petty revenge. He knew that if there was one person who might be happy to do the blond Rita a disservice, it was Mrs. Ritchie, and he set out to charm her. "Naturally you would not have much to do with the muslin company, but when a lady is so much in society as you are, she cannot help overhearing all the *on-dits*. My interest in the lady is not amorous, I promise you," he added.

The clever green eyes looked a question at him.

"What is it, then? Has it to do with that necklace everyone is talking about?"

"Precisely."

"I'd be sent to Coventry if I said anything."

"I already know she has it. I could learn her name from any number of sources. No one need know who told me. You won't be involved."

"Well . . ."

"A hundred guineas," he said.

Pride warred with greed, and lost. Mrs. Ritchie gave up being a fine lady and said, "One fifty."

"Clap hands on a bargain."

"And remember, you didn't hear it from me. It was Marguerita Sullivan. She's under Sir Percy Kruger's protection now."

"Any idea where she keeps it?"

"No, we're not close. But if it were me, I'd have it under lock and key, especially now. I expect she knows she'd hang if she were caught with it."

"It was given to her. She didn't steal it. She has only to say she didn't know it was entailed."

Mrs. Ritchie looked disappointed to hear this. "She *does* know. Much good it does her when she can't wear it. I heard she was boasting about it when David died. 'Finders, keepers.' she said. It's the likes of her that give the muslin company a bad name."

"You wouldn't happen to know where she resides?"

"A two-by-four apartment in Soho Square, from what I hear."

"Thank you. Where can I drop you off?"

"At my place, as soon as you stop at your bank."

Devane patted his wallet. "I came prepared."

Mrs. Ritchie gave him a coy glance. "So did I, but not for this."

She pocketed her ill-gotten gains happily enough, and went shopping to ease the guilt of having fiddled a sister worker. A length of emerald-shot silk and a new bonnet proved entirely efficacious.

Lord Devane drove to Soho Square and discovered where Miss Sullivan resided, but he did not call on her then. There were arrangements to be made first. He must learn something of the woman, and make another trip to his bank in case the lady was immune to threats.

Chapter Eleven

Lord Maundley disdained to meet his victim in person and sent his solicitor to outline the steps that were being taken. Mr. Rafferty was a shady character who looked more like a Captain Sharp than a solicitor. He had black hair and eyes, and a sallow complexion. He sought an audience with Lady Camden, who was supported in this trial by Mrs. Denver and the ever-faithful Mr. Caine. With much assistance from obscure Latin phrases and other legal mumbo-jumbo, Mr. Rafferty presented his client's case, mentioning briefly that the price of the missing necklace would be taken from Lady Camden's widow's portion. When everyone was thoroughly confused, he slid a document across to Lady Camden to sign. "This is the release I have prepared," he told her.

Mr. Caine took strong objection to the diminishment of Lady Camden's dowry by five thousand pounds. "Lord Maundley cannot do this. He hasn't proven anything. Let him bring a charge of theft if—"

Lady Camden, pale and defeated, touched his hand. "I don't want to have to go to court."

"But this is an outrage! He can't just seize five thousand pounds without so much as a by your leave from the courts. Maundley is taking advantage of the fact that he is guardian of your moneys. It sounds highly irregular to me."

"If the lady will just sign this paper," Mr. Rafferty repeated, nudging it forward.

"Don't sign it, Fran," Mr. Caine said. "You haven't even read it. It may be an admission of guilt. Leave it here, sir, and we'll take it to Lady Camden's solicitor."

Mr. Rafferty sighed resignedly. He would have had a very poor opinion of them if they had not insisted on this precaution. A pity the gentleman was present. The lady, he thought, would have signed on the dotted line if she'd been alone. "This paper is designed to avoid a public charge of common thievery, but if you wish to have your man peruse it, no harm. I shall leave it with you. As to the residence, that is entirely under Lord Maundley's authority. You have been occupying the premises rent-free at his pleasure. When will it be convenient for you to remove, Lady Camden? Lord Maundley's sister wishes to take occupancy as soon as possible."

This was a blatantly transparent ruse. Maundley's sister had lived with him for twenty years. A spinster in her sixties was not likely to suddenly require a residence of her own. It was a device to lend an air of decency to the expulsion, no more.

"You can see she is not fit to travel," Mrs. Denver exclaimed. Francesca looked as if she had been dragged from her sickbed, which was not far from the truth.

"I shall be well and truly ill if I have to endure much more of this. We shall vacate the premises this week, Mr. Rafferty," Francesca said.

"There is no furniture removal to worry about. Everything belongs to Lord Maundley. We rather hoped—tomorrow?"

"Sometime this week," Mr. Caine repeated. "And if Lord Maundley wishes to send over a bailiff, he will find himself charged with—" No actual, namable crime came to mind.

"Say the day after tomorrow," Mr. Rafferty suggested, a grin growing on his sallow face.

"That will be fine," Lady Camden said.

The wretched man left, and Francesca said in a listless way, "Would you be so kind as to take the house in Crawley for us, Selby? What is the price?"

He mentioned a modest rental. "I can cover that, and as the solicitor said, there isn't much to move. I shall begin sorting my things."

"Go to bed, Fran. The servants can do that," Mrs. Denver said. She was concerned as much for Fran's emotions as for her physical health. The girl looked burned to the socket.

"Perhaps I shall just rest a little before I begin." She wrote the check and gave it to Selby.

Her legs would hardly carry her up the stairs. She felt as if the weight of the world rested on her shoulders. What would Mama and Papa say when they heard? Was there any way of keeping it from them? Five thousand of their hard-earned pounds gone with the wind because she had married a wastrel, against their wishes, and inherited a rapacious, evil father-in-law along with him.

Escaping from London seemed more tempting by the moment. Before long, she was lying on her bed, gazing at the ceiling. London was horrid, and the most horrid person in London was Lord Devane. If she remained here, the best she could hope for was offers similar to his, but probably less generous. Oh, there were a few decent men, of course. Mr. Irwin had been very nice, but he was not the sort of man a lady would want to marry. Not that he had offered. And not that she could even conceivably drag a good man's name through the mud. Her eyes closed, and she fell into a feverish slumber.

Within half an hour Mr. Caine returned from the real estate agent and met with Mrs. Denver. "The house in Crawley has already been taken," he said. "I've brought a list of other possible places. With only two fifty a year to live on, it looks as if Fran will have to settle for an apartment."

"Fran detests apartments of all things," Mrs. Denver sighed, and accepted the list. "Nothing is available until the first of June," she announced after reading it through twice. "We have to be out of here the day after tomorrow. That is two expensive weeks to put up at a hotel, along with the servants . . . I don't know how we will manage."

"Mary would be happy to have her at the Elms. There is plenty of room for you, too, Mrs. Denver. Ronald, her husband, has a good-size place. And with young Harry to distract her, it might be the very thing for Fran. She was mighty taken with the baby the one time she saw him. I would invite her home to my place, but it is so close to White Oaks, and there would be no end of talk if she moved in there."

123

"It is not to be thought of. Mary's place will do nicely. Will you write her?"

"I'll do it this very minute, and send my man off with the letter. And I'll speak to my solicitor about this release Rafferty left as well. Scoundrel." He left to write and dispatch the letter and discuss the infamous release with a Mr. Duncan.

Mr. Duncan was neither dishonest nor stupid. He first listened to Mr. Caine's verbal account of the case, asking an occasional question. Next he read the document through with interest, giving an occasional grunt of dissatisfaction. While he read, Mr. Caine stood at the window, gazing with unseeing eyes at the street below, while he swayed to and fro.

When he had finished his perusal, Mr. Duncan said, "I cannot recommend Lady Camden sign this unless she wishes to incriminate herself. It is an acknowledgment that she took the necklace. It gives Lord Maundley permission to deduct its price from her moneys. Is that what she wishes?"

"She certainly does not wish to sign an admission of guilt. She didn't take it."

Mr. Duncan did not rub his hands in anticipation, but he gave that impression. "Ah, well, then the matter becomes more complicated. If you wish me to undertake the case, I shall set up a meeting with Mr. Rafferty."

"By all means. Lady Camden is willing to pay the money, but only to avoid scandal and bother. She is not ready to confess to a crime she did not commit."

"Yes, payment without prejudice, but I think we can do better than that for the lady. Paying is tantamount to admitting she is at fault. Maundley hasn't a hope in hell of proving she took it. He didn't see her. No one saw her. It is his word against Lady Camden's. Where are his unbiased witnesses, after all these months? Where is his proof of possession? Who, except himself, will stand up and say Lord Camden was a man of unblemished character? So long as there is a shadow of a doubt—"

"But Lady Camden is most eager to avoid dragging the dirty linen into court."

"Bah! So is Maundley. He is too stiff-rumped to want his own family name on public parade. He hoped to get his hands on her money on the quiet. It will never come to court. Maundley is shamming. At the very worst, and I have no intention of letting it come to the worst, my client may have to go snacks on the price of the thing. Perhaps a thousand guineas."

Mr. Caine smiled to hear this news, and hastened back to Half Moon Street to discuss it with Mrs. Denver. "I expect Mr. Duncan is very dear?" she asked.

"He isn't cheap, but he won't charge anything like five thousand guineas, and there is the principle of the thing to consider as well."

"Yes, except that the stain will always cling to Fran. No smoke without fire, folks will say."

Mr. Caine found himself in the unusual position of cheering up his companion. "She won't hear them, Mrs. Denver. She'll be safely away from it all. And it will be only a nine days' wonder before something else comes along to distract society. Some lady will leave her husband, or kill him, or her lover, and the ton will forget Lady Camden. Why don't you run up and tell her the good news? It will ease her worries."

"I just looked in. She's sleeping, so I shan't disturb her. You have been so very kind, Mr. Caine, and so helpful. I truly don't think we could have endured this without your assistance."

"Always happy to help. I sent my man off to Mary with a note. He'll bring back her answer. It is only a formality. Mary will be delighted to have her. You can prepare to leave the day after tomorrow."

"Forty-eight hours to be got in somehow."

"Less than that," he said bracingly. "We shall leave at the crack of dawn."

"And there is all the packing to do. You are coming with us?"

"For an escort. And I would like to see Mary and Ronald, too. And of course my godson. From there, I shall go home—to the country, I mean."

"We've pretty well ruined your Season. I am sorry, Mr. Caine."

"Think nothing of it. The Season is usually a dead bore, to tell the truth. I don't know why I bother coming. Perhaps I shan't next year."

He left, and Mrs. Denver set the servants to work packing the trunks for their removal and tidying the house. She felt a strong inclination to remove every ounce of flour from the bin, and the potatoes from the cellar, except she would not sink to Lord Maundley's level.

Francesca came downstairs for dinner, and was somewhat cheered to hear of the new developments. Yet she was not so cheered as her companion thought she should be. Something more seemed to be bothering her.

"I daresay you regret having to leave the gaiety of London at the height of the Season?" she asked, angling for information.

"I can hardly wait to get away."

"You will be able to take a tidy little house somewhere, Fran. We shan't be stuck with a crabbed apartment now."

"Yes, that is a relief. I do like to have a garden. And best of all, I shan't have to confess to Papa that I lost his money—my dot, I mean."

"When the dust settles, you will meet some nice gentleman—"

"Never again," Francesca said, chin jutting with determination. "Twice was enough."

"Twice!"

Her cheeks turned pink, and she said in confusion. "I have been ill-treated by two men: Camden and his father."

"Oh, I see. For a moment there I wondered if you meant Mr. Irwin." She peered suspiciously across the table.

"Certainly not! He has been a good friend, and I am grateful to him. He has been nearly as helpful as Mr. Caine, during the brief time that I have known him, I mean."

Mrs. Denver didn't smile, but she was cheered to see, or imagine, an interest in Mr. Irwin. She wondered if Fran had expected an offer. "Perhaps Mr. Irwin will drop by this evening," she said nonchalantly. "In any case, you must write and thank him for his help, and let him know you are leaving."

"I did thank him. Selby will tell him where we are going."

Francesca chattered on to cover her near gaffe. It was the most pleasant meal Mrs. Denver had enjoyed for weeks. For Francesca, every bite was like swallowing a stone. She had promised to repay Lord Devane for his insult, and now she would not have the opportunity to do it. But at least she was getting away. It seemed she would not have to pay Maundley for the necklace, and she was looking forward to seeing Mary again.

Chapter Twelve

Lord Devane spent a day doing his homework before confronting Marguerita Sullivan in his attempt to recover the necklace. He learned it was her patron's custom to call on her at eight each evening. He was at her apartment in Soho Square at seven-thirty. Sir Percy Kruger was high in the instep. He would not tolerate such grave misdeeds as thieving in his mistress. Devane had decided on using both the carrot and the stick. He would frighten her by explaining the outcome if she was caught with her ill-gained treasure: holding stolen goods was a punishable offense. She could not wear the thing, and she could not sell it. By holding on to it, she would acquire the reputation of a grasping woman, which was as harmful to a lightskirt as to a lady, perhaps more so. She would lose her present patron, and have difficulty in finding another.

Threats would weaken her resolve, and if they failed to do the trick, he would sweeten the pot with a bribe of three hundred guineas. If all else failed, he was determined to go to the limit. He arranged with a friendly judge to have a warrant sworn out to allow a search of Miss Sullivan's premises. He took the warrant and an officer of the law with him, to prevent Miss Sullivan from removing the necklace from her house.

The outside of the building gave no idea of the baroque opulence within, with gilt, crystal, and red plush everywhere. Sir Percy did very well by his piece. She had no need of the necklace. Her toilette, too, was of the first stare. She was a petite blonde, very ladylike, very pretty, and not at all stupid, though she affected an air of vulnerable simplicity that seemed to work very well with the gentlemen. Her eyes widened in guileless wonder as Devane emptied his budget, and she did not fail to recognize the significance of the Bow Street Runner standing aloof in the corner and the document he held in his fingers.

"I don't understand such long words as you use, Lord Devane. Misappropriate? What does that mean? You must know, Lord Camden gave me that little necklace as a token of his esteem." A flirtatious fluttering of the lashes accompanied her speech.

"Lent, surely. The necklace was not his to give. It is entailed."

"What does that mean, exactly?"

"It means it now belongs to Lord Maundley, until his remaining son reaches his maturity. Not a good gentleman for you to tangle with."

"But who is to pay me for it?" She pouted.

"No one. You are holding stolen property, which is a crime in itself."

"Surely not when I had no idea it was entailed," she shot back. She quickly recovered her slipping

130

innocence and added, "David said nothing of its being entailed."

"That was certainly wrong of him, but two wrongs do not make a right. It is not David who will be on trial. It is you. The court can make a case that you were aware the necklace was stolen. Why else have you not worn it? I notice you do not hesitate to wear Sir Percy's gifts."

A necklace of sapphires sparkled at her throat. Nervous white fingers played with a fan as Miss Sullivan conned her options. "Sir Percy is fiercely jealous. He likes me to wear only his gifts."

"He would be very displeased to have his mistress involved in a scandal involving another man."

She knew this was true and decided she must resort to tears. The fluttering fingers rose and shadowed her eyes. Sniffles began to escape her pretty lips. "Oh, whatever shall I do, Lord Devane? Truth to tell, I have heard a rumor—no more—that the necklace belonged by rights to Lady Camden. I have been wanting to return it, but could hardly call on her."

"You might have used an intermediary. Sir Percy, for instance."

"He knows nothing of this wretched affair."

"Shall we keep it that way?" Devane suggested in the tone of a conspirator.

She gave a helpless but withal an encouraging smile. "That might be best. There will be no scandal?"

"If you write a very pretty note to Lord Maundley explaining the misunderstanding, there will be no public scandal. He won't be eager for the world to know his son was a scoundrel. A scoundrel with excellent taste, if you don't mind my saying so," he added with a gallant bow.

She smiled softly and said, "Would you care for a glass of wine, Lord Devane, while my woman gets the necklace?" She pulled the cord and gave the woman who answered it instructions to bring the diamond necklace in the blue velvet box. When the box was in Devane's hands, she said, "Perhaps the man from Bow Street can leave us now?"

"Shall we just get your letter of explanation first?"

Miss Sullivan went to a desk in the corner of her saloon and wrote her note of explanation and apology.

Devane hastily scanned the note and put it in his pocket. "Wait for me outside," he said to the officer, and accepted a glass of wine from Miss Sullivan.

"It is a great relief to have this business settled so amicably." She smiled. "Whose behalf are you acting on, Lord Devane?"

"Lady Camden's."

"Ah. Is there some possibility of a match between you?"

"Anything is possible. I would appreciate it if you not mention it to anyone yet."

"Then you would not be taking Mrs. Ritchie under your protection?" she asked, hiding all her glee under a show of nonchalance. She had heard of that outing in the park and had a fair idea where Devane had gotten his information.

"It is not the time for me to be thinking of that sort of thing."

"I'm sure we all regret the loss," she said, peering at him from the corner of her eye. There was nothing to be gained here, but at least Mrs. Ritchie, the spiteful cow, hadn't snared this prize.

Devane finished his drink hastily and rose. "I see

by your toilette that you are going out for the evening. I shan't detain you further. It has been delightful making your acquaintance." He fingered the three hundred guineas in his pocket, wondering if he should offer a pourboire for her help. As he noticed the sparkle of sapphires, and the rich appointments provided by Sir Percy, he decided the money could be better spent elsewhere, and took his departure.

The next stop was Lord Maundley's, where he learned that his lordship was at a night meeting of the House of Lords. Devane wished to atone for his scandalous behavior to Lady Camden by taking her his explanation and a letter of apology from Lord Maundley. That, he hoped, would reinstate him in her good graces, or at least make further visits possible, to fully heal the breach.

As Maundley was unavailable, Devane had no option but to wait till morning. He spent a quiet evening at his club. Mr. Irwin was not there, so he played for only an hour before leaving. Going to a ball or rout had no appeal for him that evening. There came a time in a man's life when he had had a surfeit of meaningless parties. His visit to Miss Sullivan had disgusted him with lightskirts. He was ready to settle down, and the more he thought about it, the more convinced he became that no one suited him as well as Lady Camden.

Her brief and innocent attempts at dissipation he could well understand. He even approved. He liked a dash of fire in his ladies. She was no milk-and-water girl, to let a man ride roughshod over her.

While Devane recovered the necklace, Lady Camden prepared for her move to Surrey to visit Mr. Caine's sister and her family. She did not expect to hear from Devane again, and sincerely hoped she would not, yet each time the knocker sounded, her heart went into violent palpitations. But it was only Mr. Irwin, come to say farewell, or Selby, come to announce that he had heard from Mary, and she was eager for the visit. He wanted to arrange their time of departure the next morning.

"The earlier the better," Francesca said, and meant it.

The Elms, Mary and Ronald Travers's estate in Surrey, could be comfortably made by afternoon if they left early. There were dozens of last-minute chores to be done. Outstanding bills had to be paid, appointments cancelled, books returned to the circulating library. Mr. Caine volunteered his assistance in this last chore, and also in purchasing a gift for Harry. At eighteen months Harry had already displayed an interest in horses, and Mr. Caine bought him a finely carved and painted horse.

Caine took dinner with Francesca and Mrs. Denver that evening, as he had sent his man back home to prepare for his arrival there in a few days' time. He found that one pessimist at the dinner was enough and tried to cheer Francesca by repeating her lawyer's opinions. "Mr. Duncan is virtually certain it will never come to court, and once the necklace turns up, there will be no blame attaching to you, Fran."

"Unless people think Maundley forced me to return it, to avoid prosecution," she replied. "I *do* wish we could have recovered the necklace. That would have proved my innocence."

Mr. Caine shook his head. "It is like drawing teeth to get a word out of a lightskirt. Dealing with such creatures was never my long suit. I wouldn't know where to begin."

"You did more than anyone could reasonably ask," Lady Camden assured him. "And I shall be eternally grateful. What a wretched nuisance I have been to you, and so ungrateful. I don't know why you bothered with me, Selby."

"My pleasure, I'm sure," he said, blushing, and hurried along to a different matter. "I am having a last visit with Duncan at his house this evening, as soon as I leave you. I'll ask him about taking legal steps to recover the necklace. There might be something he can do. With a lawyer waving an injunction or some legal paper before their eyes, the muslin company might be more forthcoming."

"That will be something for the long term," Mrs. Denver said. "Meanwhile, we'll be well out of it all."

"Yes," Francesca said, and tried to smile.

But when Selby left, and she was alone in her room preparing for the move, she felt again that reluctance to leave. She consoled herself by thinking of the future, when the necklace would be recovered and her name cleared. Perhaps she would return then, and meet Lord Devane somewhere or other. She would look right through him, as if he were a dirty pane of glass. But it was cold comfort. She wanted to do much worse than that to him. She wanted to revile and humiliate him as he had shamed and insulted her.

In spite of rising at seven-thirty the next morning, and in spite of the utmost haste and bustle, it was nearly nine by the time the house was put to rights and the carriages drove out of London, Mr. Caine's leading the way. By ten they were into wooded country, away from the clamor of the city. As they proceeded through a series of delightful villages, where children played cricket on the greens and ancient churches lifted their spires into the blue sky, Francesca felt the peace of calmness descend on her battered spirits. She should never have stayed in London after David's death.

Her thoughts went forward to the Elms and Mary, her oldest and dearest friend. The travelers stopped for lunch at Croydon, and by midafternoon they passed through Reigate. The Elms, just skirting the North Downs, was four miles beyond. Mr. Caine pointed out where Ronald Travers's property began. Neat tenant farms hugged the bank of a stream, and dairy cattle harbored beneath trees, seeking shelter in the heat of the afternoon. The Elms sat on a mound, visible half a mile away.

It was a stone house formed of three cubes, the largest protruding in front, the two smaller ones recessed on either side. The elm trees that had given it its name provided beauty and shade. It was not a lovely house, and not nearly so grand as the Maundley estate, where Francesca would eventually have resided had David lived. After her troubles she could think of nothing more peaceful and satisfying than living here, with a good husband and a young family, sharing the simple country pleasures and duties. All else was mere vanity.

Her life, till now, had been useless. She had been a toy doll for David to outfit in finery and show off to his friends, and when they had all seen her, he bought a new doll. Never again would she become involved with a man of fashion. If she ever remarried, it would be to a solid, sensible farmer like Ronald Travers.

Here, in this idyllic spot, with the only sounds the smooth rumbling of the carriage wheels blending with the lowing of cattle and the raucous caw of the rooks overhead, the future did not seem utterly hopeless. As the two carriages proceeded in state up the drive toward the house, Mary came flying out to meet them. Francesca hopped down, and the two young women embraced warmly.

"Let me look at you!" Mary exclaimed. "You look peaked, Fran. We'll soon get the color back in your cheeks, and a little flesh on your bones. Oh, and look at your bonnet! How lovely! The latest crack in London, I daresay." Over her shoulder she welcomed Mrs. Denver and her brother, Selby.

Fran regarded her old friend and saw a total contrast to herself. While she had been wasting away to a hagged skeleton by late nights and worries, Mary had blossomed into satisfied motherhood. The results of her settled life were to be seen on her rosy cheeks and full figure. Her gown and her hairdo would have caused a snicker in the polite saloons of London, but they did not cause a snicker in Francesca. She felt stupidly overdressed, especially for the country. It was at her friend's sparkling eyes and bright smile that she gazed enviously.

"You look wonderful, Mary. Where is Harry? I want to see my godson."

"He's having his afternoon nap, but he'll be down soon. Come inside. Cook has prepared a special tea. Your old favorite, gingerbread and clotted cream. That will fill out your figure. Mind you, you might not want it quite as full as mine. Ron says I am a proper armful, but I expect you think I'm fat."

"No, just right."

They went inside arm in arm, chattering like

schoolgirls. Mrs. Denver and Mr. Caine exchanged a mute look of satisfaction. This visit was an excellent idea, the look said. The feeling was strengthened over tea. Francesca had not eaten so heartily in weeks. Ham and Tewksbury mustard and plain bread seemed sweeter than cake because of the company. And though she was already satisfied, Francesca had to try the gingerbread and clotted cream for old times' sake.

"And now we shall have the scion of the family brought down," Mary said proudly.

At eighteen months, Harry was walking. He had his brown eyes and dark hair from both parents, but his mischievous charm was all his own. Within minutes he had enchanted all the guests by the simple expedient of messing cream and cake all over his dress and laughing in delight at the unexpected treat. He was coaxed to say his few words—Mama, Dada, booboo, and tata.

"We'll have him saying *Fran* before your visit is over," the beaming mother promised.

Ronald was busy on the estate, but was back by dinnertime, another jolly meal, during which Francesca ate like a ploughman. "It must be the trip that gave you such an appetite," Ronald said. He was a country man with no airs or graces about him, but he possessed a handsome face and figure, and enough liveliness to please his family and friends.

"No, sir, it is your excellent produce. We don't get such lovely fresh food in London," she explained.

After dinner the ladies left the gentlemen to their port, but a good gossip between the old friends would have to wait till Mrs. Denver retired, which she soon did, claiming fatigue after the trip.

"And now you must tell me all about Maundley and the necklace," Mary said, eyes brightly eager. "Selby gave me only the merest hint in his note."

To this intimate friend, closer than a sister, Francesca left nothing out of the telling except the name Lord Devane. It felt good to empty her budget and say all the mean things she had been bottling up.

"What a perfect wretch your father-in-law is! Mr. Travers would never treat me so shabbily."

"It is David's fault, Mary. That is the fact of the matter. Papa was right. I should never have married him. My head was turned by his handsome face and his air of fashion, and, I suppose, the title. I was a fool. You are the wise one."

"Here I have been envying you when you wrote about all the balls and plays."

"Vanity, vanity, all is vanity in London. I am cured. What I see about me here is what I want." The charm had fled from fashionable friends, and from their ornate, gilt-trimmed mansions stuffed with worldly wealth. Mr. Travers's home showed every sign of prosperity without the ostentation of noble houses. It was large enough, comfortable enough, good enough—when the occupants were so obviously in love and happy.

"Then I shall just have to get busy and find you a new husband," Mary said impishly.

"I have decided to be happy as a widow."

"Oh, Fran! What fustian! You know you want a husband. You don't want to grow old alone. You should raise a family."

"I would like a child. Perhaps you're right. But

there is no hurry. I have taken a house nearby. It will be ready in July. Next time I marry, I shall take my time, and know who and what I am marrying."

"I had known Ronald fifteen years. There were no horrid surprises. He is perfectly satisfactory."

"Well, I don't think I want to wait fifteen years!" Francesca laughed.

"Are you forgetting Ronald has a cousin whom you have already known for ten years?" Mary asked with a sapient glint.

"Arthur Travers, you mean?"

"Yes."

Francesca smiled pleasantly, but something in her balked at the idea of marrying an Arthur Travers. He was just what she had been claiming she wanted. A good, sensible farmer of excellent character and possessing a prosperous estate. She mentally added another requisite to her list. The gentleman must be someone she could love. That, she saw, was going to be the problem.

Chapter Thirteen

Lord Devane, becoming impatient with Maundley, ran him to ground at Whitehall and handed over the necklace, along with the note from Miss Sullivan. He watched as Maundley fingered the diamonds and read the note a second time. His face showed neither pleasure to recover his goods nor sorrow at the trouble he had caused his innocent daughter-in-law. The only discernible emotion at first was anger. "This is some scheme set afoot by Lady Camden," he said.

"You are mistaken. Lady Camden is not yet aware that the diamonds are recovered. I have undertaken this on my own."

Maundley wanted to call Devane a liar, but did not wish to go quite so far. His most intimate friends had been horrified at his treatment of David's widow. The braver of them had even hinted that Lady Camden might be telling the truth. He was not entirely surprised at this outcome, but he was grief-stricken.

"That's it, then. My son was no better than he should be," he said, chewing back his feelings.

"That is not quite it, sir. I realize you are shocked to learn the truth about Lord Camden, but you really must call off your lawyer. And as you are a gentleman, I'm sure you will wish to apologize to Lady Camden, and ask her forgiveness for the unconscionable manner in which you have abused her."

A fiery flash of anger leapt from the man's tired eyes. "If she'd been a proper wife, none of this would have happened."

"It is my understanding that Lady Camden was a very proper wife, and indeed a proper widow until she learned of Camden's carrying-on. I know this is hard to take, but wronging your daughter-in-law does nothing to lighten the blow." He would have said more had he not been aware of Maundley's deep distress. This was not the time to harass him, but he meant to get that apology to take to Francesca. To his relief, Maundley suggested it himself.

"Yes, of course. I'll write to Lady Camden at once. As you are acting on her behalf, even without her knowledge, perhaps you would deliver my apology."

Devane bowed formally. "That was my intention, sir."

Maundley wrote his stiff note, and with a pang of conscience added a mention that Lady Camden must feel free to return to Half Moon Street if the move was inconvenient. He assumed Devane was aware of her going and her new address. He also wrote a note to his solicitor, telling him to abandon the case. He gave the former to Lord Devane to deliver. "You will know where to find her, I expect," he said.

"I do. Thank you, sir."

Maundley did not reply in words, but just nodded, as a man in a trance. Devane hopped into his curricle and darted immediately to Half Moon Street. Maundley's sister was to inhabit the house for a few weeks, for the looks of things, and it was her servant who answered the door. "Lady Camden?" she asked, startled. "Why, she's not here. She's moved."

Devane's dismay was hardly greater than his shock. He had been anticipating the moment when he handed that letter to Francesca. A dozen times he had lived in imagination her initial anger at seeing him, then her wonder as she read the letter, her growing gratitude and joy, and, finally, her repentance. He counted a good deal on her repentance to heal the breach. "Could you tell me her new address?"

"I have no idea where she went."

"Perhaps if you asked your mistress," he said, impatience arising at every delay.

The servant went off, but was back in a moment. "She doesn't know either. No forwarding address was left," she said.

"Perhaps Lord Maundley ..." he mumbled in confusion.

"He don't know. She didn't tell anyone."

"I see." He dampened down the rising impatience and returned to his curricle.

Mr. Irwin and Mr. Caine were his likeliest helpers in this fix. He had already learned Irwin's address. Unfortunately, Mr. Irwin was not home. Grimly determined, he got Caine's address from Irwin's butler and darted over to the Albany, a row of bachelors' apartments off Piccadilly. There was

143

no reply, which seemed odd. One would have thought the butler would answer the door even if the master was out. He called next door, and was told that Mr. Caine had left town.

"When will he be back?"

"Not this Season. He's given up the apartment."

"Thank you."

The remainder of the day was wasted entirely in talking to friends who had no idea where either Lady Camden or Mr. Caine had gone. Devane's frustration mounted higher at each failure. It was not till that evening that he learned the mysterious destination. His informant was Mr. Irwin, run to ground at Brooke's. Devane dashed to his table for an interview. Mr. Irwin seemed to be intimate with all the details of the case.

"Mr. Caine has taken Lady Camden off to the country while he fights the legal matter out with Maundley's solicitor, Rafferty. Rafferty tried to get Lady Camden to sign a release of half her dowry, but Caine is awake on all suits. That would be as good as an admission she had stolen the bauble. He hired Duncan, an excellent chap. Perhaps you know him?"

"Yes."

"Things are looking up. She may get away with paying only a thousand."

Devane saw his glory diminishing before his very eyes. It seemed to him that for a purely disinterested friend, Mr. Caine was putting himself to a deal of trouble on Lady Camden's behalf. The man was obviously in love with her. "She will pay nothing. The ladybird in question returned the necklace to Maundley today," he said angrily.

"You don't mean it! Who was she?" Irwin asked.

"The name was Rita something," he replied vaguely. "What, exactly, do you mean by saying Caine has taken Lady Camden to the country? Do you mean her own home, or his? . . ."

"No, no, she wouldn't want to go to her own home, and he could hardly take her to his bachelor's place."

"She could go with her chaperone if an engagement has been announced."

"But it hasn't. It was his married sister that Caine mentioned. A Mrs. Travers."

"Do you have the address?"

"No, I didn't think to get it, but Mr. Caine is to write to me. It's in Surrey."

"Thank you, Mr. Irwin. You have been very helpful, as usual. I wonder if I could impose on you for one more thing? If you would be so kind as to let me know the address as soon as you hear from Mr. Caine."

"Certainly, Lord Devane," he said, frowning in curiosity. "Mind you, he may not write for a few days."

"A few days!" It seemed he was never to find her. "Have you any idea what part of Surrey Mrs. Travers lives in?"

After much head scratching and thinking, Mr. Irwin thought he had heard Caine mention Reigate. "Couldn't swear to it, mind, but I think he mentioned Redhill being so convenient, and having such good shops. Yes, I'm sure he said something about Reigate Castle, now that I think of it. What used to be Reigate Castle, I mean. Nothing but rubble now, I believe. Is there an old Gothic arch there?"

"A Gothic archway was erected a few decades ago."

"That's it, then."

"You don't know the name of the estate?"

"It had something to do with trees—White Oaks, perhaps. No, that is Lady Camden's ancestral home."

"Poplar, mulberry, cedar . . ."

"That don't ring a bell, but you'll find it, Devane. There cannot be that many trees near Reigate. Places named after trees, I mean to say. Look in the parish records."

"Yes, an excellent idea."

Devane drove directly home, planning his next approach to Francesca. He was no longer precisely a knight in shining armor, but at least he had outdone Mr. Caine. He had actually recovered the cursed necklace, and had Maundley's apology in his pocket, whereas Caine had only hired a solicitor. Devane regretted that he had told Irwin the case was closed. He might hear from Caine and relay the news, stealing his hard-earned thunder. But Caine didn't have Maundley's apology, and if he didn't write to Mr. Irwin for a few days . . . Then, too, Irwin might not reply immediately.

Eagerness for Francesca's approval was a spur to his actions. He wanted to be the one to tell her himself, to see her face when she heard the news, and read that letter. If he left for Reigate at once, he could be there before morning. He might even find her by afternoon. He called his valet and groom and ordered them to prepare to leave immediately. It would mean driving in the dark, but he'd take his carriage, and try to get some sleep along the way.

Lord Devane's servants were too well trained to object verbally, but by various delaying tactics they showed their displeasure in being yanked out of the house in the middle of the night. His valet made a tarrying business of preparing his lordship's clothing and packing. "How long a stay shall we prepare for, milord?"

"Three or four days."

"Will you require hunting clothes?"

"One does not go to Reigate to hunt, Hudder."

"Buckskins and topboots, or—"

"Breeches and Hessians."

"Will you require evening clothes, milord?"

"Of course I will. They have evenings at Reigate, don't they? I shall also require shirts and cravats and stockings and small cloths. Good God, one would think you had never packed a bag before."

Hudder took this outburst for an indication he had gone his length, and proceeded with the packing. Next it was the groom's turn to inquire what carriages were needed, and what mounts.

"I plan to travel in my traveling carriage," Devane said with heavy irony. "Hudder and a footman can follow in the curricle. I may need a footman."

"Will you be wanting a mount?"

"No. Just the traveling carriage and my curricle."

It was an hour before the carriage was ready and Devane made comfortable with a pillow and blanket, to try to catch a few hours' sleep. As the horses clipped along in the blackness of the night, Devane closed his eyes, but he knew sleep was not going to come easily. He let his mind roam over the past days, wondering how he had made such a muddle of what should have been a perfectly simple affair.

How had he, a gentleman of broad experience, ever mistaken Francesca for anything but a proper lady? Her great crime was to have gone to the Pantheon. There was scarcely a lady in London who had not done so. She, in her inexperience, had gone with a whelp who chose a public place to try to hound her into marrying him. Oh, yes, and she had worn a patch on her breast. A very attractive patch. A very attractive breast, come to think of it.

As for the rest of it, it was Maundley's tale that she had stolen the diamonds that did the damage. Damn the man. Yet one had to pity him, learning that his beloved son was a knave and a scoundrel. One heard the younger scion—Horton, was it—was more stable. Lady Camden's reputation was not quite ruined, but it was under fire. Her running away at this time was at least prima facie evidence of guilt. That was ill-done of Caine to have rushed her out of town.

She must be made to see this, and be brought back. With himself as an escort, she would soon be reestablished to not only respectability, but preeminence. He would remove her from that pack of Camden's she had been running around with. He did not say the word *marriage* even to himself, but it was in the back of his mind. Who better than a husband to guide her, to show her the ropes and polish her town bronze? Eventually he slept, and not much later was awakened by the crowing of a rooster. Darkness had required a slow pace, and they were just approaching Reigate. The rising sun edged the eastern horizon in crimson.

It was pointless to begin his search at five o'clock in the morning, so he hired a room at the Swan and caught a few hours' sleep. At eight he rose, bathed, dressed, had a hasty breakfast, and set out for the closest church to peruse the register. He began with the parish church of St. Mary Magdalen, and by lunchtime he had visited all the local churches. He had encountered more than one Travers family, but none that met his requirements. Unfortunately, he had not thought to learn Mr. Travers's first name, but he knew at least that he was looking for a Travers fairly recently married to a Miss Caine.

He bought a map, and at lunch he pored over it, noting with dismay how many places he had to visit. Gatton, Leigh Church, Charlwood Church, and a little farther afield, Buckland, Betchworth, Brockham Green. This could take days. He would divide the territory up and send his servants into the countryside to examine the church registers. He would snoop around town. If the Traverses lived nearby, they must visit the local shops. Mr. Travers must execute some business here in the city.

In the afternoon he began his search at the stable yards, thence on to the inns. At times he felt he had gained his end. "Mr. Travers? Oh, aye, he stables his rig here from time to time. It's old Mac you mean, and not Ted Travers?"

"A youngish fellow, married to a Miss Caine."

"Oh, now, I don't know as I'd call Mac young. Seventy something, and young Ted is fifty if he's a day. But a young fifty. Still spry."

"Does Ted have a son?"

"All daughters. Spinsters, all five of them. It's the squinty eye that destroys their looks."

Next he tried the inn stable yards, with a similar lack of success. He spoke to real estate agents and lawyers and doctors. It seemed the professionals and businessmen of Reigate made a living on people named Travers, but never the Travers he wanted. His minions returned with a similar lack of success, and by dinnertime Lord Devane feared Mr. Irwin had led him astray. He was temporarily downcast, till it occurred to him that the marriage must have taken place in Miss Caine's parish. He was unclear as to its precise location, but at least he knew it was close to White Oaks, the Wilson estate.

It was quite by accident that he finally made the discovery that evening in the tap room at the Swan. He went in to have a few ales before retiring, and found himself sharing a table with Mr. York, a prosperous farmer. The farmer mentioned his business almost as soon as he had introduced himself. "I've been down at the Elms, buying a brood milcher from Mr. Travers. He has an excellent herd."

Lord Devane's glass hit the table with a thud. "Mr. Travers? The Elms! By God, that's it!"

Mr. York looked at him obliquely. "You know Mr. Travers? His herd is certainly the best hereabouts, but I own I am surprised his fame has spread all the way to London."

"Is he married to a Miss Caine?"

"I'm afraid I didn't meet his wife. She had company visiting her. An old school friend, Lady Camden."

"You must tell me how to reach the Elms."

"Why, it is no secret, milord. You just take the road southeast out of town and continue five miles."

Lord Devane rose, looked at the head-and-shoulders clock on a shelf, and sat down again. Nine-thirty was too late to leave for a call. He wouldn't be there before ten. But tomorrow morning he would see her. "You must allow me to buy you a drink, Mr. York."

Mr. York looked at his full glass and said, "Why, thank you. A little later, perhaps. Tell me, milord, as you are in the House, what is the official opinion on this war? With Austria on our side, and Blücher leading the Prussians, things are looking up, eh?"

"Things are definitely looking up."

Chapter Fourteen

Upon first awakening the next morning in a strange room, Francesca was momentarily confused. The window was on the wrong side of the room, and the curtains . . . Then memory washed over her, and though she was happy to be at Mary's, she felt that the past was still not quite behind her. The necklace affair had still to be settled. It bothered her, too, that she had skulked away from town like a thief. Yet, if she had remained there, she would be confined within walls on such a beautiful day as this. Not even the walls of the house on Half Moon Street, but in some shabby rented apartment.

She threw back the coverlet and went to the window. Sunlight streamed on fields as green as emeralds. The branches of the elm trees swayed gently, suggesting a mild breeze. She lifted her eyes to the sky, and saw a fat cloud shaped like a lady's bonnet. She wanted to go out barefoot and run through those meadows while the dew was still on the grass. She wanted to gather wildflowers, and to wade in that silvery ripple of stream weaving through the meadow. The water would be icy and fresh. She pushed aside the city gowns in her closet and chose a simple rose-sprigged muslin.

Mary was already at the table when she went belowstairs. "What would you like to do today, Fran?" she asked while Francesca examined the sideboard. She chose eggs, bacon, toast, and even tried some of Ron's favorite, fried potatoes. "I have the whole day free. Tomorrow the ladies church group is meeting here in the afternoon to discuss the bazaar, but today we are free. Would you like to drive into Redhill? Tom isn't using the carriage, and they have some very nice shops."

Francesca brought her plate to the table and began eating. "Let's not go shopping. I'd like to just putter around outdoors. Walk through the park, talk to the cows, and take the jig for a little drive in the countryside this afternoon."

Mary tilted her head aside and smiled at her. "Just do the things we used to be so eager to get away from, you mean? Do you remember, back at White Oaks, how you used to crave the excitement of the city?"

"I'm cured. I've had a surfeit of city excitement. It was horrid, Mary."

"It all sounded so wonderful in your letters. You mean the last while was horrid, once you found out about David."

"I suppose that is what I mean. Now I just want to rusticate, and let my bruised spirits heal. Show me your chickens. You are alway boasting of them. I must admit their eggs are delicious. They taste so fresh."

"Just gathered this morning," Mary said proudly.

"Cook sprinkles a little chopped chives in them. The herb garden is my prerogative, too."

"As soon as we've admired your chickens, we'll tour your herb garden."

"Exciting!" Mary said, and laughed, but she was pleased to see that her old friend had not grown beyond such simple pleasures. She had been entertaining the fear that Francesca would have turned into a grand lady, but her toilette and her interests belied that fear. "You must not think I am utterly sunk to raising chickens and chives. Your arrival is timely. There is an assembly tomorrow evening. Not the big do in Reigate, but Mrs. Huddleston is giving a small private assembly. I shall have a rout, too, while you are here."

These functions meant little to Francesca, but she sensed that they featured large in Mary's social life, and expressed the proper interest.

During the day the ladies reestablished their easy footing of previous times. It was pleasant to drive along the country lanes in a pony cart, an umbrella warding off the sun's punishing rays. While they were gone Selby was busy inventing other pleasures for them. He rooted out the croquet mallets, balls, hoops, and pegs, and set up a course in the park. Mrs. Denver was called upon to make the fourth player, and the afternoon was idled away with this game. Mary served lemonade and cake in lieu of afternoon tea.

In the evening Fran helped make purses for the church bazaar, and fended off Mary's idea of driving over to Fernbank to visit Mr. Arthur Travers later in the week.

"Very well," Mary said, "but I give you fair

154

warning, I shall invite him to dinner on Sunday, so prepare your best bib and tucker."

The next day was similarly free of any but the most simple diversions. In the morning Mary had her way and drove Fran and Mrs. Denver over to Redhill to visit the shops. With an air of daring she suggested they dine at the inn. Mrs. Travers was told, when they returned to the Elms, that a gentleman had called for Lady Camden. He hadn't left his name, but he was from London. He said he would return in the afternoon.

"It must be Mr. Irwin," Francesca said when the message was relayed. "Are you sure he did not leave his name?"

No, but his description, "a tall, good-looking city gentleman," sounded like Mr. Irwin.

"I am happy he is coming, for I shall be busy with my church group for a few hours this afternoon," Mary reminded her. "Is he a beau, Fran?"

"No, he is really Selby's friend, but he helped me with that wretched necklace business. Perhaps he will take your place for another game of croquet while you attend your meeting."

Lord Devane, who had called at the Elms that morning, figured that Lady Camden should be back from her expedition to Redhill by three, and at five minutes to three his curricle rolled up the drive of the Elms. Lady Camden had gone to the garden with a book to read while awaiting her caller. She was not reading, however, but sitting with the book on her lap, daydreaming, when the servant approached and said, wide-eyed with alarm, "It's Lord Devane to see you, milady."

The book fell from Francesca's fingers, and her

face turned as white as paper. "How dare he! I am not at home to Lord Devane. Pray tell him so."

"But he's a lord," the servant replied in consternation. Showing him in had been harrowing enough. How was she to turn him away?

"He is a thoroughgoing wretch. If he makes any trouble, call Mr. Caine." She rose and went into the house, not to grant Lord Devane an audience, but to make sure he did not charge his way in.

The servant went, trembling, to do as she was bid. "She says to tell you she's not at home. Sorry, milord," she said, red in the face.

Devane's black brows drew together in a quick frown. He took a deep breath, wanting to lash out at someone. Was this his reward for dashing about the city and countryside to help Lady Camden? "Pray tell her it is extremely important. A matter to her advantage," he said through thin lips.

The servant ran Lady Camden to ground in the morning parlor. Something drew Francesca to Devane like a magnet, but this was as close as she could go without being seen. Devane's message was delivered. Lady Camden pokered up and replied, "Pray tell Lord Devane that my idea of advantage is quite at odds with his. I have no desire to see him, *ever*."

"He said it's important. Extremely important."

"Not to me," she said, and turned to stride from the room.

The servant returned to the door. "She says your idea of advantage and hers are at odds. She won't see you, milord, *ever*."

Devane's nostrils flared dangerously. He fingered the letter from Maundley and seriously considered the feasibility of forcing his way in. "May I speak to Mrs. Travers, if you please?" he said.

"She's at a meeting. In there," the servant added, tossing her head toward the saloon. The buzz of female voices at work was audible behind the door.

"Is it a cabinet meeting, that she cannot be disturbed?" he demanded.

"No, a church meeting. I'll get her."

Mrs. Travers was summoned with the important words, "Lord Devane would like a word, ma'am. Very insistent, he is."

"Lord Devane?" Mary said, puzzled. "Who can he be?"

"A friend of Lady Camden's, only she won't speak to him."

Mary was highly curious, and not entirely displeased to be summoned by a lord in front of her friends. "I had best see what he wants," she said, and went to the door.

During the brief hiatus Devane had assumed his most beguiling expression. He could usually charm the ladies if he had a mind to, and it seemed he was going to require a conspirator in this house to reach Francesca. Mary looked at him and saw an extremely elegant gentleman wearing an intriguing smile. Authority exuded from him like spring sap from a pine tree. He performed a bow of exquisite grace and said, "You cannot be Mrs. Travers! I expected an older lady."

She blushed and smiled prettily. "I am indeed Mrs. Travers, Lord Devane. How can I help you?"

"Perhaps if we could have a moment in private?"

She led him into her husband's study. "It is about Fran, Lady Camden, I believe?"

"Precisely. We have had a—falling out," he said

with a sad grimace. "She refuses to see me, but I have a most important matter to discuss with her. Perhaps if you told her it is about the diamond neck—" He came to an abrupt halt.

"I am in her confidence in the matter," Mary said simply.

"Oh, good." He smiled again, more naturally. "I feared I had put my foot in it there. I have news that I think she will wish to hear."

If there was one thing Mary knew about Fran, it was that she was as stubborn as a mule. If she had refused to see this terribly handsome Lord Devane, she would not be dissuaded. "If you would care to tell me the nature of the news . . ."

Devane fingered the letter from Maundley. He wanted to be there when Francesca read it, but as that was impossible, he handed it to Mrs. Travers. "I shall await her reply," he said.

Mary went into the hall, where she met her servant. "Where is Lady Camden?"

"She's gone up to her room," the servant said. "Do you want me to take that up to her ladyship?"

"No, I shall take it myself."

She darted upstairs, tapped at the door, and rushed into Francesca's room, waving the letter. "Fran, what is amiss with Lord Devane that you are treating him so shabbily?" she scolded. "He is terribly handsome, and I know he is in love with you. He sent this note. It's about the diamonds."

"He is in love with himself," Francesca retorted, but she took the letter and tore it open. That gratifying range of emotions Devane had been imagining did not occur. She frowned and read it twice, then a third time.

"I have this day recovered the Maundley necklace. I apologize most sincerely for thinking you were involved in its disappearance, and humbly ask your forgiveness. Naturally I shall inform my solicitor of this turn. You must feel free to return to Half Moon Street if you so desire. Sincerely, Maundley."

Francesca looked bewildered. "Maundley has recovered the necklace," she said, still wondering how it had happened. "How did Devane come to know of it? What has it to do with *him*, that he is delivering me this letter?" she demanded as curiosity gave way to annoyance.

"I wager it was Devane who recovered it. You must see him, Fran. He has come all the way from London."

"How could he have recovered it? He would not even believe it was stolen."

"Why don't you ask him? He is waiting downstairs. I think it uncommonly sly of you never to have mentioned his name."

"I told him I would not see him—ever. How dare he— oh, he is the most exasperating man. I shoudn't be in the least surprised if he bought the thing back from David's mistress on purpose to put me in his debt."

"Is that where he wishes to place you? I wonder why," Mary said archly.

"Because he would like to watch me cringe and grovel. He has outfoxed himself if that is what he has done. Pray deliver my thanks to Lord Devane, but I am indisposed. I cannot see him." She rose and paced the room, fighting back the urge to run downstairs as fast as her legs could carry her.

"Is that all you have to say?"

"What more is necessary for the simple delivery of a letter?"

"Oh, Fran." Francesca lifted her chin and looked out the window. There was no misreading her mood. "Very well, but I think you are being unnaturally stubborn."

Mary returned below, determined to discover the whole course and nature of her friend's relationship with Lord Devane. The ladies' group must wait. This was more important, and the ladies had plenty to gossip about in the meanwhile. It was not every day that their meeting was enlivened by such romantic goings-on.

She smiled pleasantly as she entered. Devane was not seated, but pacing impatiently. She noticed his eyes eagerly scanning the empty space behind her in hopes of seeing Fran there. "Lady Camden is very grateful to you for delivering that letter, sir. She asked me to convey her thanks. May I offer you a glass of wine?"

"Thank you."

Ronald kept but an inferior sort of claret in his office, to aid his nocturnal battle with the bookkeeping, but she poured two glasses and they both sat down. "What did she say?" he asked at once.

"She was very pleased, as I said. She was curious to learn how it came that *you* were delivering the note from Lord Maundley."

"I insisted he write it when I took the necklace to him."

"You took it to him! But how exciting, Lord Devane. I am sure Fran does not know *that*. How did you recover it?"

He was easily tempted into relating the tale of his chivalry, sure that it would all be relayed to Francesca. "It is not a story I can tell without blushing, for Lord Camden was not exactly . . ."

Mary shook her head sadly. "I know. He was a sad trial to her—but posthumously, of course, which made it worse in a way. She could not repay him as he deserved. Fran felt David had given the jewelry to a—a female friend," she said, coloring modestly at such licentiousness. Devane noticed, and thought how innocent these country girls were. "She could hardly credit a thing like that, you know, being reared so carefully as she was. Her papa is a byword for puritanism."

"Yes, Lord Camden did give it to a female. I investigated and discovered the recipient, paid her a visit with a Bow Street Runner and a search warrant, and the thing was done."

Mary's eyes were large with admiration. "But how did you discover the woman's identity? Selby—my brother, Mr. Caine, has been trying to discover that for months."

"One has to know what palms to grease," he said, making little of it.

"So much bother and expense as you have been to. You must think very highly of Lady Camden," she said leadingly.

"More highly than she thinks of me, I fear."

"Perhaps when I tell her what you have told me ... But there is no point in thinking she will cave in without time to change her tune. Fran is most stubborn."

A small, wan smile tugged at Devane's lips. "And has the devil's own temper," he added.

"Are you staying in the neighborhood for long?"

"Until she condescends to see me," he replied with an air of injury. This won an approving nod from his hostess.

"There is an assembly tomorrow evening. Mrs.

Huddleston, the hostess, is in my saloon at this moment. If you would care to attend, I am sure she would be delighted to have you."

"Fran can hardly throw a book at my head in a polite saloon." He smiled. "Would I be imposing too rudely to accept your generous offer?"

Mary was so bowled over by Devane that he could have imposed on her for anything but her son. "You'll be the making of her do. We don't get many fine lords. Lady Camden *and* Lord Devane—this one will go down in history."

"Let us hope it is not recorded as a battle. Perhaps we should keep it a secret that I will attend."

"Yes, an excellent notion. We don't want Fran digging in her heels and staying at home. Where are you putting up, Lord Devane? I would invite you to stay with us, but under the circumstances . . ."

"No, no, it is not to be thought of. I am at the Swan, in Reigate. I can be reached there if Lady Camden wishes to see me before the assembly."

"Yes, if I can talk her out of her sulks." She felt easy enough with Devane to add, "What did you do to get in her black books? Fran is mulish, but she usually requires a good cause to set her off."

He rose and bowed. "I must leave you ladies some subject for gossip, ma'am. Ask your friend. The secret is hers to tell or not, as she wishes. But I might as well admit, she had good cause to distrust me. If she reveals my disgrace, you might deliver my heartfelt apologies. I was wrong, and I deeply regret any pain I have caused her."

Mary thought that was very prettily said and smiled her own forgiveness without hearing the crime. She gave him directions to Mrs. Huddle-

162

ston's house and said he would undoubtedly be receiving an invitation at the Swan that same day.

Very little church bazaar work got done that afternoon. Mary caused as much sensation as a simple country matron could wish when she returned to her saloon. The precise nature of Devane's call was not revealed, of course, but when she asked Mrs. Huddleston if she would mind very much sending Lord Devane an invitation to her assembly, no one cared why he was there. They assumed, and were not discouraged in the assumption by Mrs. Travers, that it was an affair of the heart involving Lady Camden.

From there, the subject turned to quick additions to the assembly to make it worthy of two noble guests. The two fiddlers and a pianoforte must be augmented by a cello, and the orgeat with champagne. Every lady in the room wished to dart over to Redhill for new feathers or gloves or silk stockings so the meeting broke up quickly, and Mary was free to go upstairs as she had been longing to do.

Francesca had been studying that letter from Maundley and trying to conjure Devane's part in it. He had bought the necklace from Rita, thinking to force her into becoming his mistress. And to go chasing her into the country, barging into her friend's house—the more she thought of it, the more she feared it might actually come to a duel.

She was ready to do battle with someone when Mary came tapping at her door. "I finally got rid of the ladies," Mary said, dropping onto the bed.

"What did Devane say?" Fran asked in a quiet voice, but a voice laden with mistrust.

"I got the whole story from him. He was eager to

tell it." She relayed Devane's part in the affair, diminishing nothing of his concern and efficacity.

"He didn't *buy* the necklace back? You're sure he didn't pay for it?"

"Indeed he did not. Lord Devane is no Johnny Raw. He is up to all the rigs. He got a search warrant and a Bow Street officer to go with him. And he made Maundley write that apology, too."

"That was certainly well done of him," Fran admitted, somewhat mollified. "I expect I should write a note, thanking him."

"He is putting up at the Swan in Reigate for a few days. We could drop around . . ."

"No! No, but I must write a note."

"Why do you not wish to see him, Fran?"

"We do not get along. We would be sure to come to cuffs before the meeting was over."

"What do you usually come to cuffs about? I thought him charming, and very conversable."

"He can be charming and conversable; he can also be impossible."

Mary gave an impatient *tsk*. "I wish you would tell me the truth. Whatever it is, Lord Devane admitted he was wrong, and he told me he is very sorry."

Fran smiled softly. "Did he say so? Well, perhaps I shall write a very nice note."

Mary jumped up from the bed. "We have time to get to the Swan before dinner."

"Oh, no. I mean to write. If Devane wishes to pursue the matter further, he must tuck his tail between his legs and come to me."

"He did not strike me as a gent who would be much good at truckling, Fran. Don't let this stubbornness of yours go too far. I expect there are plenty of ladies on the catch for Devane in London. Well-dowered debs," she added, to remind her friend she was a widow. Widows were not held in such high esteem as maidens.

"Good gracious, I was not implying I expected an offer."

Mary got up from the bed. "Weren't you? Now I see why you were not eager to drive over and visit Ron's cousin. I must own, Lord Devane quite puts Arthur in the shade. Now I must go. Nurse will be feeding Harry, and I never miss that."

She danced out the door, her mind full of the assembly and Fran's romance, and, of course, of Harry. She meant to teach him to say *Fran* before her friend left.

Chapter Fifteen

The evening at the Elms was quiet to the point of tedium. Francesca's chief diversion was to write her note to Devane, and when it was done, to sit and chat and sew smocks for the bazaar. It was the sort of evening she had been accustomed to at White Oaks before her marriage, but after the gaiety of London, there was no denying she felt the lack of liveliness.

Mrs. Denver had been informed of Lord Devane's message, as had Selby, and there was unrestrained joy between those two, though one would not guess it to see them chatting quietly by the grate. "Fran can return to London now if she wishes," Mrs. Denver said. "Maundley has offered her back the house."

"She has already hired the cottage. Best to stay away from that Babylon on the Thames. See how much calmer and happier she is here."

Mrs. Denver, more familiar with Francesca's moods, thought her calmness held an edge of ennui, but she was too polite to say so. Mrs. Denver was fully alive to the advantages of marriage to such a gentleman as Lord Devane. Having heard nothing of his various outrageous acts, she felt his fast reputation must be false. His behavior in rescuing Fran was not the act of a man of bad character. It had every appearance of a man in love.

"If she had a proper escort and did not hang out with her old set, she could manage well enough in London. I do believe she's learned her lesson. She's had her wings trimmed; she would not fly so high a second time."

"I shouldn't encourage her if I were you," Selby cautioned.

Mary had had the card table set up temporarily in the saloon to hold her sewing materials. "Would you like me to send that note to the Swan with a footman, Fran?" she asked as she set a neat stitch in a blue smock.

"There is no hurry. Tomorrow will do well enough. You mentioned Devane is remaining in the area a few days, I think?"

"Yes, that is what he said."

"You'll be sending in your eggs tomorrow, Mary," Ronald reminded her. "No point making two trips."

Mary was eager to get things moving, but she seldom countered Ronald's pronouncements. She satisfied herself by discussing toilettes for Mrs. Huddleston's assembly instead. "What will you wear?"

Fran considered it a moment. "For a country party, there will be no need of a grande toilette. I shall wear my blue crepe and pearls."

"Oh, but the ladies will all expect to see London fashion, Fran." *And so will Lord Devane,* Mary added silently to herself. "Do not hold back for fear of outshining the rest of us. Be as grand as you wish."

Mrs. Denver, listening in, said, "You could wear your new green silk with the gauze overskirt. Your pretty green slippers will add a touch of London to your outfit."

"And, of course, long kid gloves," Mary suggested.

Francesca divined that she was expected to lend cachet to her hostess by being as grand as possible, and acquiesced to it with a resigned smile. It all seemed rather pointless, since there would be no one but farmers to see her.

They retired early and rose early the next morning, to spend another quiet day, enlivened by preparations for the assembly. In the afternoon they drove over to the vicarage to deliver half a dozen smocks for the bazaar. "Ronald has the carriage, so we will have to take the pony cart. You don't mind, Fran?" Mary asked.

"Why should I mind?" Fran laughed. "I wish you would not treat me like a guest, Mary."

Lord Devane also spent a quiet day. He received his two notes, one inviting him to Mrs. Huddleston's assembly, which had to be answered. The other required no reply. It was from Francesca, and it was as polite as she could make it without accusing herself of encouraging Devane. He read it with some satisfaction, though he had rather expected an invitation to call.

In the afternoon Devane took his grays out for a spin. His drive took him, not quite by chance, in the direction of the Elms. When he saw a pony cart in the distance, he assumed it was carrying some country girls, and paid little heed except to draw his curricle toward the edge of the road to leave them room to pass.

Francesca had recognized him. There was no mistaking that proud head, and his team of bloods. Her heart raced, but other than a slight heightening of color, she revealed no alarm. "I believe that is Devane," she mentioned to Mary. "Pray do not stop the rig. Keep going."

"But this is your chance to—"

"Keep going!" Fran ordered in a thin voice.

It was not till they were actually passing that Devane discerned the identity of the occupants. It was too late to halt his team, but he slowed them down as much as he could, lifted his hat, and said, "Good afternoon, ladies" in a loud, friendly voice.

Fran would not allow herself to turn around, and forbade Mary from doing so, yet she knew as surely as she knew her name that Devane was looking back to see if they were stopping. His team's pace had slowed nearly to a halt.

"Why would you not stop?" Mary asked when all danger of a roadside chat had passed.

"*He* did not stop. Why should *we*?"

"He slowed down. He would have stopped if you had let me. He didn't recognize us at first."

"I said what I had to say in my note."

Mary had a fear for the success of their meeting at the evening assembly, and said, "I hope you would not be so brusque if you happened to meet Lord Devane at some public place."

"That would depend on how he behaved," Fran replied nonchalantly. She rushed on to speak of other things, and Mary consoled herself that Devane would undoubtedly behave as he ought that evening.

Mrs. Huddleston's assembly began at eight o'clock, to allow her guests to arrive before the sun set, even if they had to drive home in the dark. The party from the Elms arrived shortly after eight. With a total of forty guests, forty-one including Lord Devane, it was one of the neighborhood's larger private parties. The house was lit from top to bottom, and flares burned in the driveway to welcome the callers. Within, tall vases of flowers in the hallway where the Huddlestons greeted their guests lent a festive air. The new arrivals were not announced, but just shook hands with the host and hostess, and went in to hand their coats and pelisses to the footman before proceeding into the small ballroom.

The four corners of the ballroom bristled with potted palms, and on a makeshift platform the musicians sat tuning their instruments. The ear-splitting sound of tuning fiddles pierced the air. The room was already well filled when the Traverses and their guests entered. Mary was gratified at the attention her guests caused. Fran looked lovely in a misty sea-green gown with a spangled overskirt. Mrs. Denver had arranged her coiffure in a sophisticated do, pulled straight back from her face and swirled up behind, held in place with pearl-tipped pins. Matching pearls at her throat were her only jewelry. The ladies were ogling her as hard as the men were, to see what new styles they could pick up.

A quick glance around showed Mary that Devane had not arrived yet. She introduced her guests to the neighbors, and as the first set began, Ronald's cousin, Arthur, came forward and asked Francesca to stand up with him. Francesca had been trying to imagine being married to Arthur, or someone like

170

him. She could not prevent herself from comparing his country bow, his country barbering and tailoring, to Devane's sleek style. She knew it was foolish to place much weight on such trivialities, and tried to look beyond them.

His conversation was sensible, but after a brief compliment on her toilette, he spoke of his cattle and farm, of the weather and local doings in a way that lacked any aura of romance. The best she could think of him was that he would make a wonderful husband—for someone else.

As the set ended she began to peer around the room in hopes of discovering some more interesting partner. She found none, but as Arthur Travers led her to the side of the room, Ronald approached. She must have a set with Ronald, might as well get it over with. It was a country dance. Any meaningful conversation was impossible as the dancers rollicked up and down the line. Francesca glanced around to see who Mary was with, and stopped dead in her tracks. She was with Lord Devane! What was he doing here?

Ronald grabbed her arm and pulled her along the line. "Are you tired out already, Fran?" He laughed. She gave a weak smile in return. For the rest of the set she scarcely knew what she was doing. The steps were automatic to her; she performed them mechanically while her mind raced back to Devane. Who had invited him? Did he know the Huddlestons? Had Mary arranged this? Why had she not been warned? What would she say when he came to her? There was no doubt in her mind that he would come to her.

But when the next set began, it was Selby Caine who advanced. Devane was standing up with a pretty young blonde. There was no necessity for reticence with Selby. "What is Devane doing here?" she asked.

"As he is in the neighborhood for a few days, Mrs. Huddleston invited him to her do. I believe she met him at Mary's place yesterday. You'll have to thank him for recovering the necklace, Fran. He has pulled your chestnuts from the fire, so you cannot go on glaring at him."

"I am not glaring at him! I wrote and thanked him."

"You must thank him in person as well, since he is here. You need not fear he'll hound you. Don't tell him where you'll be living. I told Mary not to mention it. He'll be back in London by next week, so you can be civil for one evening."

When the set was over, Selby led Fran toward Devane. Whatever Devane's feelings, he concealed them like a diplomat, and said, "Good evening, Lady Camden. A pleasure to see you again." He bowed gracefully.

Francesca performed a small curtsy and returned the greeting.

"The musicians take a break after the third set. The refreshment parlor is across the hall, if you are thirsty," Mr. Caine said, and took a discreet departure, leaving Devane and Francesca alone.

Devane drew her aside as the crowd surged in an amorphous body toward the doorway. "Would you care for a drink?" he asked.

"A little later, after the crowd has thinned." She summoned up her courage to say what had to be said. "I want to thank you for your help, Lord Devane. I cannot imagine why you went to so much bother on my behalf."

"Can't you?" She felt as if those dark eyes were looking right through her. The breath stopped in her lungs, and she could think of nothing to say. "I behaved abominably. I hoped that by recovering the necklace I would recover your esteem as well. *Recover* is hardly the correct word, as I don't believe I ever actually had it. *Win* your esteem, shall we say?" There was a playful air about him that eased the strain of the meeting.

Francesca was relieved. This was the sort of conversation she was accustomed to now, and a reply came easily. "Not only my esteem, but my undying gratitude, sir. You cannot know what a strain the whole business has been."

"I have some idea. I can see, at least, that you are looking much better than the last time I saw you. Is a comparison less odious when we compare someone to herself?"

"So long as you imply an improvement, then I for one shan't cavil with it. Mary told me a little about how you recovered the necklace, but I would like to hear all the horrid details sometime."

"I am eager to boast of my prowess—but perhaps this is not the time and place."

"You're right. I was surprised to see you here, Lord Devane."

He waggled a shapely finger and laughed. "No, Lady Camden. You were shocked. I feared you would reduce your square to a shambles when you spotted me. You looked as if you had seen a ghost."

"I was shocked, I confess."

"It was shockingly forward of me to cadge an invitation to the party of a stranger, but how else was I to have a word with you, when you refused to see me?" There was a shadow of accusation in his expression, and Francesca felt the weight of it. "I thought, when you received my explanation, that you would grant me a short meeting."

"I didn't realize when I read Maundley's letter that you were instrumental in the matter. I thought you were just delivering his note."

"And you were not curious enough to inquire?" The face gazing at him was the face of an uncertain child. He felt an urge to pat her head and say, "There, there. It's all right, Fran."

"Actually, I feared you might have bought the thing back from Rita," she said hesitantly.

His quick frown of confusion soon cleared to comprehension. "I have no right to be angry, since I brought that on myself. My intention, however, was to rectify the wrong, not add to it."

"You did offer to pay for it, when—"

He grasped her hands and squeezed them. "Don't remind me. Let us bury the past and see if we cannot be friends."

"Yes, let us drink to that—if we can fight our way to the refreshment parlor." She peered out the door and across the hall. "The crowd seems to be thinning."

As the meeting was going well, Devane wanted to keep her to himself a little longer. "You wait here. I'll bring you a drink." He led her to a chair by the wall and went to get wine.

Francesca welcomed the moment alone to recover her equilibrium. She was beginning to acknowledge what she had been trying to conceal from herself for some days now. She found Devane dangerously attractive. If she had much to do with him, she would soon be in love. In love with another man who was the mirror image of David. Devane had mistresses. He was a city buck who would not be faithful to his wife for long. And besides, he probably had no interest in marrying her. "See if we cannot be friends," he had said.

She drew a troubled sigh. It seemed she was in the impossible position of not being able to love the gentlemen who would make good husbands. She had a perverse taste for rakes and scoundrels. The sane course would be to not marry at all, then. She had her dowry intact again, since Maundley had dropped the case against her. She and Mrs. Denver could be happy in the quiet of the country, performing good deeds, enjoying such simple social outings as this. She would miss the excitement of the Season, but her recent experience had taught her that was not too high a price to pay for peace.

When Devane returned, he found her pensive, aloof. "When will you be returning to London?" he asked a moment later. "The reason I ask is that I hope you will permit me to call on you there."

"I will not be returning, Lord Devane."

He turned on his most charming smile. "I think you were unwise to leave. The gossip will have died down by now, however, and if you return, your friends will welcome you."

"Friends who are so easily lost are not worth regaining. I will not return, ever."

"Forever is a long time. I enjoy rusticating from time to time, but I find the country palls after a while."

"I was born and reared in the country. It won't pall on me."

"You seemed marvelously at home in the flesh-pots of London, ma'am." His smile held an echo of her flaming past.

"Perhaps ladies like me, who are a trifle susceptible to temptation, are best off at a distance from all that."

Devane cast a dubious look at her. "Surely we are all susceptible to pleasure." Sets were beginning to form in the middle of the floor. He took her empty glass and put it aside. "What susceptible ladies require is the proper escort. Shall we join this set?"

Nothing more was said about London, and as Devane did not ask Francesca where she meant to live in the future, she did not either have to tell him or appear coy by withholding the information. When they parted at the end of the set, he asked if he might call on her at the Elms, and she gave her gracious consent.

"How long will you be staying with the Traverses?" he asked.

"For a few weeks. You, I understand, will be returning to London soon?"

"Not for a few days. I look forward to seeing you tomorrow."

They did not have another dance. Francesca didn't know whether she was relieved or disappointed that he did not ask her for a waltz, but she knew that her heart was sore to see him having the dance with an attractive redhead. No matter, he would be leaving in a day or two. He could not break her heart in two days.

Chapter Sixteen

Francesca did not delude herself that she was indifferent to Devane, but she had no intention of falling in love with him. And the best way of avoiding that was to make sure that he recovered from any little partiality he felt for her, and removed himself from the neighborhood as soon as possible.

What had attracted him in London was the dashing widow who tried for attention by foolish tricks of toilette and flirtation. All that was put aside. Knowing he was coming to call, she went to the bottom of her trunk and took out a simple blue dimity gown she had had before her marriage. No collar, lace fichu, brooch, or necklace enlivened its severity. She bound her raven tresses in a tight chignon and went belowstairs to breakfast.

Her hostess was too polite to express her astonishment, and soon concluded that Fran meant to make her toilette after luncheon. Fran liked to make herself useful around the house, and would not want to wear her fine silks to the chicken yard, or while sitting on the porch shelling peas for dinner.

As they rose from luncheon, Fran said to Mary, "Shall we take Harry out to the park for some fresh air before his nap?"

"I'll do it, Fran. You will want to change before Lord Devane comes."

"I am not changing. And I do not wish to see him alone. Let us take a blanket out under the trees."

Mary looked at the severe coiffure and plain dimity and exclaimed, "Oh, Fran, are you trying to give him a disgust of you?"

"Certainly not. If he is disgusted with me, that is his affair."

Mary noticed, however, that her friend glanced into the mirror and frowned. "Do I look that horrid?" she asked uncertainly.

"Certainly not, but you looked much more elegant last night."

"That's all right." Francesca was not unhappy with the image in the mirror. This quiet style was not unflattering in its own country way. What it took away in elegance it added in a suggestion of maturity and even sobriety. During her few days in the country she had gained some color in her cheeks, and the anticipated visit lent a glow to her eyes.

Mary shook her head and sent off for Harry and a blanket. They sat under a spreading mulberry tree, and took turns running after Harry, who was interested in the gardener working near the house. When Lord Devane's yellow curricle came dashing up the driveway, Francesca raised her arm and waved. He stopped and called, "Will you come for a drive, or shall I stable my rig?"

"Stable it," Fran replied.

"The stables are at the rear, Lord Devane," Mary added. It was hardly necessary, but she wished to play her role with all propriety.

The gardener came forward and led the rig around. Devane hopped down and joined the ladies. If Francesca thought she was putting him at any disadvantage by this domestic sort of meeting, she soon discovered her error. After the greetings and a mention of last night's assembly, Devane lifted Harry onto his shoulders and took him for a ride, making a lifelong friend of Mary, who was greatly honored to see her son disporting himself on such handsome noble shoulders.

"For a bachelor, you seem very much at home with children, Lord Devane," she complimented him.

"I am an old hand at entertaining children. I have two nephews and a niece. Mind you, I am not much good with dolls and juvenile tea parties."

"What age are your nephews and niece?" Mary asked, and for the next ten minutes the conversation was between the two of them. Fran entertained Harry by helping him move his wooden horses and soldiers about. This undemanding chore left her time to think that as Lord Devane had asked to call on *her*, it was odd he chose to hold all his conversation with Mary. But she was interested to learn he was a brother to Lady Morgan. Fran had met her, and she seemed amiable.

"I'll ask Cook to send us out some lemonade—or would you prefer ale, Lord Devane?" Mary said later.

"Ale, if it's no bother. Lady Camden is aware of my partiality for ale," he said, trying to draw Francesca into the conversation. She gave a vague smile. "No, don't trouble to take Harry with you. We'll mind him." Harry tried to follow after his mama, but Devane lifted him up and brought him back. He sat down by Francesca and leaned against the tree trunk, his legs extending on to the blanket. Harry was held between his legs, handing Devane his toys one by one. "Your friend seems very nice," he said to Fran.

"She is. We were always close. I am happy to see her so comfortably settled." Her eyes turned to Harry, the cause of half of Mary's joy.

She felt again that pang at not having had a child of her own. How different things would have been if she had. She would not have stayed on in London. It was the great, yawning emptiness and pain of her life that she had tried to fill up with spurious pleasure. So foolish, really.

She glanced up, and saw Devane gazing at her, sympathy gleaming in his eyes. His clean-cut jaw was limned against the tree trunk like a cameo. Black, satiny hair caught a trembling ray of sun and glinted blue and purple and amber, reminding her of a peacock's feathers. His lips opened in a rueful smile. "You're young, Francesca. There is no reason you shouldn't be equally comfortably settled."

She shook her head. "I do not think of marriage. Once was enough."

"There are different kinds of marriages. I don't mean to sound like a vicar, but I think you had the misfortune to make the wrong kind for the sort of lady you are. You could have had no notion what to expect in London society. On the surface all is glamour and glitter, but there is a darker underside to it. Unfortunately, you stumbled into that darker realm, through no fault of your own."

His eyes studied her, unblinking, trying to find in this simple country girl an echo of the dashing lady with the patch on her bosom. The transformation was startling, but what startled him more was that he found both equally enticing. To his consternation, he also discovered that Lady Camden was making no efforts whatsoever to attract him. There was no coy hint for an objection in her statement against marrying.

"Unfortunately, the sort of lady I am has poor judgment where gentlemen are concerned. I was never really attracted to the local beaux. I always wanted something more, the excitement and glamour of the ton, but when I achieved it, I found it illusory."

He felt some slur on his own behavior in this speech, again delivered in a straightforward way. "Only the young and inexperienced are taken in by the glamour. When you return, you will be wiser, and leave the rakes and rattles to the debs." As he spoke, he kept accepting Harry's offerings, which now formed a pile on the blanket beside them.

Francesca picked up a horse, and Harry snatched it back. "I do not plan to return. I think I mentioned that last evening."

Her bland manner annoyed him. Her rejection of London annoyed him. It was not his whole life, but it was an enjoyable part of it. "Six weeks is the correct length for the Season. Six weeks out of fifty-two to relax and enjoy society. I spend most of the year at the Abbey, my estate in Kent. It is close enough to London that I can run home during the Season if I feel a surfeit of high living. And close enough that I am always available at Whitehall if some emergency arises."

Francesca tilted her head and smiled at him from under the brim of her straw bonnet. "I cannot picture you in the country, somehow."

The eyes, lifted to her, gleamed with some negative emotion, and when he spoke, his voice was strained. "It doesn't take that much imagination. You see me now, enjoying the country. Did you think I spent twelve months a year in dissipation?"

Before she could reply, Mary returned, accompanied by a servant bearing a tray. The drinks were passed around, and the servant took Harry back to the house for his nap. Devane turned to his hostess and engaged her in conversation, determined to show Francesca that he was not an idle fool interested in nothing but women. "That's a fine-looking herd you have, Mrs. Travers. I was admiring them as I came here. Guernseys, I see. I have mostly Ayrshires myself."

"Ronald's breeding them with some Jerseys—for the higher butterfat, you know."

"I've bought a few Brown Swiss, thinking to get both milk and beef, but my steward tells me I should be introducing a few Jerseys. What sort of yield do you get from yours?"

"You should talk to Ronald about that. You'll stay to dinner, I hope?"

His eyes slid to Fran, who was gathering up Harry's toys and refused to look at him, though she listened eagerly, half hoping he would refuse and half fearing it. "I don't like to impose." He looked again at Fran. She still refused to look at him, but he noticed her hand hesitate till he gave his reply.

"Do stay. Ronald would love to talk to you," Mary urged Devane.

"Thank you. I should dart back to the inn and change." The fingers holding the wooden soldier— did they tremble?

"There's no need to dress. Ronald welcomes any excuse to sit down in his buckskins. Mind you, he doesn't usually sink so low when we have company."

"Then I shan't lead him into bad habits."

The conversation returned to cattle, and after some time Mary, noticing Fran's trick of retiring from the conversation, said, "I'll just let Cook know you'll be staying for dinner, Lord Devane." She shot her friend a commanding glance as she left.

"Do you mind my staying?" Devane asked Fran.

"Of course not. Why should I?"

"My vanity led me to think you were not pleased."

"Not pleased? Pray, what has that to do with vanity?"

"It shows *some* feeling at least. I have had the impression this past half hour that you forgot I was here."

"Oh, I don't know much about cattle."

He gave a conning smile. "Nor do I, but I have a feeling I'll know a good deal before the evening is over. I know that they got me an invitation to dinner, in any case."

Francesca felt a turmoil in her chest at this leading speech, but she was determined to quell it. "Any knowledge you manage to pick up will not go amiss, as you *do*, I assume, raise cattle?"

"Indeed I do. I may prevaricate a little when the

183

occasion calls for it, but I don't lie. Would you like me to go now?"

She gave her old London shrug. "Suit yourself."

He gave her a searching look from the corner of his eye. "I don't think you want me to take that literally. What I want to do is kiss you."

She pursed her lips and looked at her fingers which were twisting like snakes in her lap. "No, I don't want that." She glanced up, and saw he was gazing at her lips. She could almost feel her own lips tingle under his gaze. "Perhaps you had best go." He smiled then in a bemused way. The curving of his lips left little dents at the corners of his mouth from trying not to laugh.

"Doing it too brown, Frankie!" he said, and reaching forward, he placed a quick kiss at a corner of her lips. "I am enchanted by your new style, but don't completely forget the other one."

She recoiled as if his lips were live coals. They left behind a burning sensation. "This is not a style!" she protested weakly.

"With a little work it could become one. The country look—yes, it has possibilities. The patch on your skirt is not so intriguing as that patch you wore at the theater, but more genuine."

She caught her bottom lip between her teeth in chagrin. She had forgotten the patch on her skirt. She had mended it herself after she tore it climbing a fence while picking berries at White Oaks years before. It was a clumsy piece of work; mending was not her long suit. "We were feeding the chickens this morning. I didn't bother to change."

"Don't feel it necessary to change for me. I, on the other hand, have promised Mrs. Travers not to lead her husband into bad habits, and must return

184

to the inn to change for dinner. Country hours, I expect."

"We usually dine at six, but Mary will put it off till seven, to impress you."

"We'll compromise. I shall come at six-thirty."

"I'll tell her. And you were going to tell me how you recovered my necklace, Lord Devane."

"Don't you think you might drop the 'Lord'?"

She nodded. "What I am most curious to hear is who David gave it to."

"It was Marguerita Sullivan. Her friends, I believe, call her Rita. Mr. Irwin kept harping on that name, now that I think of it."

"The name Rita appeared on some billets-doux David left behind. We thought she might have the diamonds." Devane scowled at such callousness. "Rita Sullivan. I don't know her, even by sight or reputation. I suppose she is very beautiful?"

"Quite attractive-looking." But she paled into insignificance beside Francesca. Lord Camden was a fool. "A blonde," he added.

"How did you recover the necklace?"

He gave a brief account of the incident, not wishing to dwell on his familiarity with the muslin company.

"How did Maundley take it? He must have been upset to learn his son's true character. I hope he keeps it from Lady Maundley."

"Maundley was very upset. I think he didn't want to believe it, but knew in his heart it was true. He must have had some idea, I should think. You are generous to worry about him after the way he treated you."

"I never knew the Maundleys very well. They judged me by the reputation I made for myself after

185

David's death. It was foolish of me, but that's all over now. So far as I am concerned, Frankie is buried." She spoke with some trace of bitterness at her own folly.

Devane cocked his head and grinned. "Let us not bury her too deep; I was rather fond of her. There is a little Frankie in most ladies. The trick is not to let her get the bit between her teeth and run out of control.

He rose and offered his hand to help Fran rise. She accompanied him to the house for his curricle. She asked the gardener to bring it around and waited with Devane till it arrived.

His last words before he hopped into his rig surprised her. "Are we friends, Francesca?" he asked in a serious way.

"Yes, why not? You have done me a great service. I cannot imagine why you put yourself to so much bother."

"I did it to expiate for the great disservice I did you earlier. I hope I have paid my debt. Don't put David's wrongs in my dish, too."

Then he hopped up, gave the reins a jiggle, and was off, leaving her alone to ponder his words. It was true she had put him in tandem with David in her thoughts, yet there were striking differences in their behavior. Devane had mistaken her for a lady of pleasure when he accosted her at the Pantheon. It was not entirely his fault; as she sadly admitted, she had looked and perhaps behaved like one. His consorting with lightskirts was not admirable, but at least he had the excuse of being a bachelor.

Perhaps he would be untrue to his wife, but she felt in her bones he would never do anything as despicable as David had—giving away a family heirloom and letting his wife take the blame for it. His eagerness to repay the wrong he had done her proved he had an active conscience. David was a hypocrite. He had been at pains to hide his doings from his parents, done it so successfully that till the day the truth was forced down Maundley's throat—and hers—they could none of them believe what he truly was.

Devane laid no claim to being a saint and allowed a streak of wickedness in others. He was "rather fond" of Frankie. The whole world knew him to be a dashing bachelor. If dashing bachelors did not suit some, they could be left alone. She found him very hard to leave alone. What plagued her was whether a dashing bachelor could make a faithful husband.

Chapter Seventeen

Devane had laughed at her mended skirt, so obviously Francesca could not appear for dinner in anything too countrified. Yet she was determined she would reveal no trace of the infamous Frankie Devlin. She chose her modestly cut blue crepe, stylish enough but not the highest kick of fashion. The shade, the pale ash-blue of delphiniums in decline, was attractive with her ivory complexion and raven hair. She brushed back her tousle of curls and bound them in a blue velvet ribbon. Some desire for distinction left her fiddling, dissatisfied with the ribbon. She chose a longer length, and tied it over her left ear, allowing the two ends to fall nearly to her shoulder. She had never seen any lady wear a ribbon in just that way.

It would set another style in London—if any lady from London were to see her, that is. She smiled at her own incorrigible affinity for attention, and would not let herself attach a pearl brooch to the ribbon. "There is a little Frankie in most ladies. The trick is not to let her have her head."

To atone for the new style of ribbon, Francesca gave up her grand late entrance and was in the saloon when Lord Devane arrived. His toilette made no concession to the country. He looked as elegant as he did when she saw him in London. There was no denying his height, and shoulders, tapering to a trim waist, made the perfect form to show off Mr. Weston's tailoring. The dramatic contrast of immaculate white collar against the black jacket and his swarthy complexion was pleasing. Although he dressed as he usually did, she sensed some new modesty in his manner. He greeted her with warm approval, and was at pains to ingratiate himself with Ronald. The best and easiest way to do so was to show an interest in dairy farming. This topic arose over sherry, and continued to dominate the better part of the dinner table conversation.

Francesca noticed Mrs. Denver and Selby listening with interested approval. Other matters were discussed as well—a few compliments to the hostess, politics, and neighborhood doings. She was happy to see Devane could make himself agreeable to any company. Surely that was the mark of the true gentleman.

After a hearty dinner the ladies left the gentlemen to their port and retired to the saloon. Mrs. Denver immediately broached the subject Francesca most dreaded. "Why is Lord Devane lingering in the neighborhood, Fran? Did he happen to say?"

"No, he didn't."

Mary laughed coyly. "I can think of one good reason, ma'am. You must have noticed he is head over ears in love with Fran."

Francesca expected a frown to pull at her chaperone's thin face, and was surprised to see only a gleam of interest. "Do you think so?" she said, speaking to Francesca.

"Of course not. And I would not welcome any advances if he did make them."

"He is not the sort of gentleman we first took him for," Mrs. Denver pointed out. "He seems a serious, almost sober sort of man. And so kind about the necklace." Mrs. Denver, of course, did not know of Devane's infamous behavior in London. "His character is respectable. Not a saint, but never one to prey on young girls."

"I always liked a streak of the flirt in men," Mary said. Both women stared to hear this coming from the lady who had married Ronald Travers. "Why don't you ask him why he lingers, Mrs. Denver? There is no point asking Fran to do it. Butter wouldn't melt in her mouth when Lord Devane is within hearing distance."

"I hardly feel it is my place," Mrs. Denver replied, "though I own I am becoming very curious."

"I'll ask him, then," Mary said pertly, and laughed. "You must distract Ronald, Mrs. Denver, for he will prose our ears off about his cattle if we leave him with Lord Devane."

When the gentlemen joined them, Mary made good her promise, and Mrs. Denver abetted her by cornering Ronald to inquire about his creamery. Mary suspected Devane would head like a homing pigeon for Fran and stationed herself nearby. He nodded and smiled at Mrs. Denver, but walked straight to Francesca.

"Have you come for a respite from discussing cattle, Lord Devane?" Mary asked. "There is no stopping Ronald once he mounts his hobbyhorse."

"I hope we did not bore you at dinner. Your husband is so knowledgeable that I forgot my manners and harped on the subject. He is selling me a brood cow at an excellent price."

"Oh! Is it cattle buying that keeps you in the neighborhood?" she asked innocently.

Devane gave her a knowing grin. "Not entirely, Mrs. Travers."

Francesca blushed like a blue cow and said, "Lord Devane is always looking for an excuse to leave London. I seem to recall your eagerness to attend country house parties in the past, Devane."

"And *your* eagerness to avoid them, ma'am." He added to Mary, "You are the only hostess who has succeeded in luring your friend from London."

"How long will you be at the Swan?" Mary asked him, and felt so uncommonly bold that she added a pretext for the question. "The reason I inquire is that I plan to have a dinner party in Fran's honor. If you will still be here in a few days' time, I hope you will attend."

"I will be delighted to come, Mrs. Travers. I am in no hurry to rush away from such warm hospitality."

Mary gave her friend a conspiratorial smile and rose. "I must see what is keeping the tea tray."

"Well, do you think I have passed muster with your friends?" Devane said frankly.

"You are an unqualified success. Why you put yourself to so much bother, I cannot imagine."

"Bother be damned. Manners are free. The cow is costing me a fortune."

Her lips moved unsteadily. "I hope it is a good cow."

"I consider it a wise investment. I must have *some* excuse for hanging on so long. You have noticed questions are beginning to arise—one might almost say expectations."

"Of what?" she asked, and immediately regretted the question. His kindling look was answer enough.

"This is a conversation that could be carried on more efficaciously in private. Will you drive out with me tomorrow?" She bit her lip and tried to think of a way of avoiding another meeting. "I must warn you," Devane continued, "I can be a perfect burr. I have every intention of sticking until I get you alone, if I have to buy every cow in Travers's pasture."

"Very well, but—" She could hardly go on to refuse an offer that had not been made. "But I do not plan to return to London," she finished lamely.

His eyes made a leisurely examination of her hair and face. He noticed the dangling velvet ribbons caressing her jaw. Another innovation in her toilette. Her heightened color revealed her excitement. "You have given up on the dairy-maid look, but I think that ribbon might catch on with the ton. Don't you miss the delights of society?"

"I have no objection to the society I find here."

"I shall grab that unwitting compliment and thank you, Francesca."

Ronald advanced toward them. "Do you want to have a look at Bessie's record now, milord? I told you I would show you the records of that milcher you're buying. You won't regret the purchase."

"Excellent." He rose at once and made his bow to Francesca, who had to smile to see the elegant Lord Devane following meekly to the library to pore over records that she was sure would bore him to distraction.

The tea was cold by the time Devane was allowed to return. Mary offered to call for a fresh pot, but he refused like a gentleman and took his leave.

Before departing, he went to Francesca. "Will two o'clock be convenient tomorrow?"

"Yes, that's fine."

As soon as he was out the door, the ladies had to hear what this was all about. "We are going for a drive. That's all," Francesca explained.

"You'll come back engaged! I know it!" Mary crowed.

Mrs. Denver smiled, and even Selby didn't frown. It was for Ronald Travers to make the final statement. "He seems like a gentleman of good, sound sense. A lady could do worse, taking into account the title and estates. A good deal worse."

Alone in her bed that night, Francesca took herself severely to account. Have I no common sense? Did I learn nothing from my first marriage? Devane was a womanizer. She could not marry him—yet every fiber of her wanted to hear an offer. Perhaps it was not going to be an offer after all. He had asked if they were friends. . . . But his glowing eyes surely held more than friendship.

She would tell him point-blank she was not interested in the sort of marriage that meant a month's honeymoon followed by a string of mistresses. London, and the Season, were out. Devane would never consent to such an arrangement. She would miss the Season herself. . . .

She hardly knew how she got in the next morning. She had some vague impression of helping Mary write cards for her dinner party and discussing a menu that included much beef and cream desserts, all from the Traverses own farm. But all the

193

time her mind was on Devane and the drive. It seemed an eternity before two o'clock finally came, and the knock at the door announced his punctual arrival.

He was met by all the party except Ronald, who was busy with his work. Francesca was annoyed that the household gave the call the solemnity of a formal visit by sitting in state in the saloon, waiting. The conversation, however, was brief and unexceptionable. The weather and the best roads for a spin were mentioned by Mr. Selby. Mrs. Denver reminded Francesca to take a warm pelisse, as she would be in an open carriage, and Mary invited Devane back for tea after their drive.

While this was going forth, Francesca surreptitiously examined her caller. A blue worsted jacket, straw-colored trousers, and shining Hessians had replaced his clothes of the previous evening without diminishing Devane's elegance a whit. She rather regretted her determination to be a country girl. She wore a sprigged muslin and plain blue pelisse. Her chapeau was a simple round bonnet enlivened with a wreath of colored flowers.

"We shan't be late," Francesca said to her hostess as they left.

The sun shone in a brilliant blue sky. Rooks soared idly amid the spreading elms, and somewhere a thrush sang. "It's a lovely day," Francesca said as Devane handed her up into the curricle.

He made a playful bow, then hopped up beside her. "I ordered it especially for you. How many mindless dandies have told you that, I wonder. You see the sort of trip it is going to be. Platitudes and politeness, until I have convinced you you aren't really a country wench, despite that hideous round bonnet. I was mistaken about the country style catching on. A lady needs the face of an angel to wear such a quiz of a bonnet. You just barely get away with it, Frankie."

"Is this your idea of platitudes and politeness, Devane?"

"I changed my mind." He gave the team the signal, and they were off. "It was that invitation to tea that did it. It shortens our outing. I had planned to drive to Dorking for tea. A private parlor seemed a good spot for a proposal," he finished with no change in tone.

Francesca sat like a nun, deaf in one ear, but her heart was racing. "Dorking is said to be in the fairest part of Surrey. We have time to go there, I think—but not for tea."

"Actually, I'm not sure that a private parlor is the best spot for a proposal," he continued as calmly as though discussing the weather. "There is something to be said for the open air. Trees, birds, flowers—all that. We'll keep an eye out for a private spot, a little away from the road, but not too close to a cow pasture."

"We could drive to Reigate."

"I noticed an apple orchard as I drove along. Does it belong to Travers, do you know?" He lifted his eyes from the road then and glanced at her, chewing back a smile. That prim face, he fancied, was the expression she wore in church.

"Or Redhill—it is said to have excellent shops. But I don't suppose you are interested in shopping."

"That won't be necessary. I have the ring with me." He did not add it had been received only that morning, thanks to a dart to London by his groom.

195

Even this telling speech was ignored, though it cost Francesca a supreme effort. "Oh, I know! Let us go to the Recreation Grounds, north of High Street. There are vaults and caverns. They have something to do with the Magna Charta, I believe."

"Very romantic, Frankie, scrambling around in a sand pit. The tale of their being associated with the barons who forged the Magna Charta is apocryphal."

"St. Mary Magdalen church, then. Lord Howard, who conquered the Spanish Armada, is buried below the chancel."

"I have already been to that church, looking for you."

"At St. Mary Magdalen church?" she asked in confusion.

"Looking for the Traverses, actually, in the parish record. Mr. Irwin knew only their last name and the general area where they live. I have been combing the countryside, looking for them. What do you think took me so long to come to you?"

She treated this question as rhetorical and said, "We could go to Reigate Priory. It was once the seat of Lord Howard—the one who defeated the Armada."

"Good God, is that a suitable spot for a proposal? You are confusing love and war."

She gave up ignoring his talk of marriage and turned on him in vexation. "There is no confusion, sir. Love leads to marriage, which leads to war between the man and wife. I have had enough of marital warfare. I am not interested in it."

They had not gone half a mile yet. No romantic spot had appeared on the horizon. Perforce, Devane continued the drive. "As we are not married yet, could we not call a truce while we discuss this like adults?"

"There is nothing to discuss. Pray, take me back to the Elms."

"Mrs. Travers will hardly have tea prepared so soon. It is the nadir of bad taste to inconvenience one's hostess. But I shall not importune you again on that subject you dislike."

For two minutes they continued in silence. Then Devane said, "I think, in your marriage, it was choosing the wrong partner that gave you such a disgust of the institution."

She tossed her shoulders. "We were not going to discuss that subject."

"We were not going to discuss *our* marriage. I am discussing yours."

"Men are all alike—and so are marriages."

"Your friend Mary would stare to hear you say so. I cannot picture Ronald Travers causing his wife a moment's grief of the sort you suffered."

She snorted. How dare he suggest she would ever marry a man like Ronald Travers? "What has that to do with you and me?" she asked, sparks shooting from her eyes.

"Very little, I hope, but it might suggest to a rational lady that all men are not alike."

"That is true, but it does not suggest to me that you have a single thing in common with Ronald. You are more like David."

"I thought as much! Now we are coming to the crux of the problem," he said, nodding to himself. "It is clearly not the careless disposition of diamonds we are discussing. I grant you that Lord Devane, bachelor, had something in common with your husband; viz., an interest in women. Lord Devane, husband, however, would be a different article altogether."

Francesca relented to the extent of granting him a small, distrustful peep. Encouraged, he pulled into the closest roadway, which chanced to be a graveled walk leading to a gate in the pasture fence. Mr. Travers owned the fields on either side of the road, and when his herd had grazed one side, he would open the gate and lead them across to graze the other. Other than a dusty tree drooping over the road, nature had endowed the spot with no particular aids to romance.

Francesca said coolly, "Different for how long? A month? Two? How long would it be before you returned to your old ways?"

Devane dropped the reins and gazed at her. "I cannot read the future any more than you can, Francesca. It is my intention to be a faithful husband. If you feel fidelity more likely in the country than in London, then I am willing to give it a try."

She looked suspicious but saw by his face that he was serious. "Would you really give up the Season for me?"

"Truth to tell, I share your concerns to some extent. You have many friends—let us be blunt—many beaux in London."

"But I would never continue with them after I was married!" she exclaimed, shocked and angry at such an imputation.

"Then why should you imagine I would?" he asked simply. "I am not a boy. I've done the town for fifteen years, looking for a lady who could fill my life as I hope to fill hers. If I wanted only a titular Lady Devane to give me a son and heir, I could have married eons ago. To speak quite frankly, and risk offending you, even now I could choose a wife less likely to cause me trouble and grief."

Reading between the lines, Francesca knew that he could also marry one much higher in society, better dowered, unwidowed, and of unsullied reputation. Many a noble lady was on the catch for Devane. "Then why on earth are you offering for me?" she asked angrily.

"Ah, did I fail to mention it? How grossly remiss of me. I am asking you because I happen to love you, and beneath that prickly exterior, I suspect you care for me."

"But you could do much better for yourself, Devane."

"I could marry some duke's daughter whom I do not love, but I could not be faithful to her. As the French duke pointed out, where there is marriage without love, there will be love without marriage. Is that what you are recommending, Francesca?"

"No indeed! You must know that is exactly what I am against."

"Then it comes down to one important question, doesn't it? Do you love me?"

It all sounded so simple when Devane said it. He could marry anyone he wanted, and he wanted to marry her. Why should he do so unless he loved her? And if he loved her, why would he want anyone else? "Yes, but—but David loved me, too, and he was not faithful for very long." Her lip trembled, and a worried frown pleated her brow.

An angry scowl pulled his brows together. "Let us not begin this way, Fran. I'm not David. Don't punish me for his sins. You married a scoundrel and a rake. I am neither one. I am a bachelor who

199

wants to settle down with the woman he loves. Will you have me, or not?"

The moment she half anticipated and half dreaded had arrived, and she was by no means sure what she should do. Devane seemed sincere. He had nothing to gain by marrying her, unless it was her companionship. If she said no, she knew she wouldn't see him again. He was too proud to grovel. And if she never saw him again, she would be miserable. The very thought of the future without him was intolerable.

"Yes," she said in a small voice. "I'll marry you, Devane." She was within a heartbeat of saying more. *But if you ever deceive me, I'll—* The words remained unsaid. It was unfair to burden him with David's legacy. It was a new beginning with a new faith and trust.

And besides, how could she speak when his lips were bruising hers in a heady kiss? His arms crushed her painfully against his chest, as if he'd never let her go. The old fears were dissipated in new love and joy. David had never kissed her so fiercely. Perhaps this passion was what he had been seeking with those other women. . . . She threw caution to the winds and threw her arms around his neck. She'd love him so much he'd never give a thought to any other woman. She'd be wife and mistress, if that was what it took.

When he stopped kissing her, his eyes looked wild and dark. A wan smile played on his reddened lips. "Lord Camden was a fool," he said. "And that is the last time you'll hear his name on my lips."

"So was I. I didn't love him as I should have, but I don't mean to give you any excuse to stray, sir."

"Let us go and see that church before we do something we shouldn't."

Francesca withdrew her arms from his neck and smiled pertly. "The church of Mary Magdalen. That seems a proper destination for such a fallen woman as I."

"I meant see the vicar, and discover the closest bishop, so that we may arrange a special license. Because if we have to wait much longer, Frankie . . ."

She peeped at him from under the small brim of her round bonnet. "One would think to hear us that we were no better than we should be."

"Oh, we are much better. We just happen to be madly in love."